Robyn's smile widened.

"We'd probably better head back, in case Mom's got company." She pulled out her phone and checked it. "Just as I thought. No service out here."

"Let's go." Rick hurried to the back of his sled and reached for the snow hook. She hadn't protested his comment. As they took the trail back, he found himself looking forward to kissing her and hoping that time came soon.

The dogs pulled them back toward the Holland Kennel yard at a smart trot. Rick believed those on his towline could have kept going all day and loved it. As the miles flew by, his thoughts drifted back to their embrace. Robyn was right—parkas weren't the best attire for courting.

Cheryl came out the back door of the house as they came to a halt and ran to where Robyn hitched her team leaders. "I'm so glad you're back!"

"What is it, Mom? Did Mr. Sterns show up here?"

"Not yet, but six of our dogs are missing."

SUSAN PAGE DAVIS and her husband, Jim, have been married thirty-three years and have six children, ages fifteen to thirty-two, and six grandchildren. They live in Maine, where they are active in a small, independent Baptist church. Susan is a homeschooling mother. She has published more than twenty novels in the historical romance, cozy mystery, romantic suspense, fantasy, and contemporary genres. She loves to hear from her readers. Visit Susan at her Web site: www.susanpagedavis.com.

Books by Susan Page Davis

HEARTSONG PRESENTS

HP607—Protecting Amy
HP692—Oregon Escort
HP708—The Prisoner's Wife
HP719—Weaving a Future
HP727—Wyoming Hoofbeats
HP739—The Castaway's Bride
HP756—The Lumberjack's Lady
HP800—Return to Love
HP811—A New Joy
HP827—Abiding Peace
HP850—Trail to Justice
HP865—Always Ready

Don't miss out on any of our super romances. Write to us at the following address for information on our newest releases and club information.

Heartsong Presents Readers' Service
PO Box 721
Uhrichsville, OH 44683

Or visit www.heartsongpresents.com

Fire and Ice

Susan Page Davis

Heartsong Presents

To Debbie,
We are so glad you are part of our family!

Acknowledgments:
Special thanks to Rhonda Gibson, Lisa Harris, and Dana
and Luann Nordine, who helped make this book possible.

A note from the Author:
*I love to hear from my readers! You may correspond with
me by writing:*

Susan P. Davis
Author Relations
PO Box 721
Uhrichsville, OH 44683

ISBN 978-1-60260-678-4

FIRE AND ICE

Scripture taken from the HOLY BIBLE, NEW INTERNATIONAL VERSION®. NIV®.
Copyright © 1973, 1978, 1984 by International Bible Society. Used by
permission of Zondervan. All rights reserved.

All of the characters and events in this book are fictitious. Any resemblance to actual persons, living or dead, or to actual events is purely
coincidental.

*Our mission is to publish and distribute inspirational products offering
exceptional value and biblical encouragement to the masses.*

PRINTED IN THE U.S.A.

one

Robyn Holland stooped over the yearling pup and worked the harness gently over his legs.

Grandpa Steve brought out two more experienced dogs and hooked them to the towline. The veteran dogs would run in the wheeler position—at the back of the team, nearest the dogsled.

The yearlings, Muttster and his littermate Bobble, wriggled and danced, eager to run in the crisp new snow with the big dogs. Robyn hooked them to the towline farther forward, each one beside an older dog who had pulled sleds for several years.

At the very front, Grandpa positioned their pair of leaders, Tumble and Max. "Everybody set?" Grandpa asked.

"Yeah, but I think you'd better let me take them around the loop once before you take over." Robyn patted the youngest dog's head and stood. "It's the first good snow we've had in weeks, and the trail's going to be fast."

"Finally."

Robyn frowned. "It won't be like pulling the ATV, you know."

"I know."

She bit her lip. Her grandfather had grown frail last winter, his arthritis keeping him from doing much of the dog training that kept them solvent. But when summer arrived and his doctor started him on a new drug regimen, he'd perked up. One of the jobs he'd enjoyed through the fall months was driving teams of dogs hitched to the Hollands' ATV. In the old days, Grandpa had used a light cart for training on dirt trails, but the acquisition of the ATV three years ago had increased their training options. It gave the dogs more weight behind them, to hold them steady during fall training, building muscle and stamina.

There was plenty of snow now, the last week in December. Grandpa seemed as eager to get out with the sled as the dogs did. He'd suffered a bad cold and hadn't driven any of the teams since they'd put the cart away in early November. He felt better now, and with plenty of snow on the ground he couldn't wait to get out on the trail again. But could he control a team of eight dogs, two of which had only minimal training?

"I'm just saying, they were frisky Saturday. Today they're excited by the fresh snow *and* frisky. That sled weighs a lot less than the ATV."

"I can handle them," Grandpa insisted.

"Oh, I know. It's just that—"

"Hey, I was racing dogs before you were even thought of." Grandpa glared at her from his place at the back of the sled. "Are you going to get the snub line, or do I need to?"

"I'll get it."

Robyn walked to the line that anchored the team's leaders to one of the few trees in the dog lot. This year's crop of puppies pressed against the link fence of their enclosure, watching the big boys. The other mature dogs also stood, panting as they gazed at the fortunate ones who'd been chosen.

She looked toward Grandpa, and he nodded. No use arguing with him, even when he was wrong. But he *had* been running dogs decades longer than she had.

With misgivings, she unsnapped the line.

"Hike!" At Grandpa's quiet command, the dogs leaned into their collars and pulled. They made a quick start. The leaders lunged forward, hauling the youngsters with them. The other dogs in the team kept pace, and the sled zipped over the packed snow in the yard, toward one of the trails they used most.

Robyn wished she had hitched up a few dogs to their old sled so she could follow along. But then Grandpa would accuse her of babysitting him.

She watched them until they were out of sight and went to get her plastic toboggan from the barn. In winter she used it to haul water and food to the dogs. She gathered up a dozen water dishes. The water froze and the dishes had to be emptied and refilled several times a day or the dogs would dehydrate.

Her mother put on her coat as Robyn entered the back door of the kitchen carrying half the dog dishes.

"Hi, honey. I'm just about to leave for work. I see Grandpa got his way."

"I couldn't stop him. He'll be all right." Robyn met her gaze and felt another flash of doubt. "He wanted to go so badly."

"He's a good trainer. He knows what he's doing." Her mother picked up her keys and purse.

"Yeah. And it will be a short run today—just a couple of miles. He'll be back soon." Robyn put the water dishes in the sink and walked outside with her mom.

They both turned without speaking toward the dog lot. The dogs barked and wagged their tails.

Robyn couldn't help smiling. "They're all so happy that we've got plenty of snow."

"Yes, it was sparse for a while there." Her mother peered toward the trail Grandpa had taken.

Robyn walked over to the male dogs' enclosure, opened the gate, and went in. She stooped to pat Scooter, her brother's retired lead dog. He was more of a pet than a team dog now, but she sometimes harnessed him with yearlings to teach them trail etiquette. Scooter rubbed against her hand and woofed.

She stroked his ears and straightened. The mountains to the north were solid white against the clear blue sky, with shadows of purple, gray, and navy delineating ridges and cliffs. Who else on earth had such a beautiful place to live and work?

"Here they come." Her mother's voice held relief.

Robyn straightened and peered toward the trail. She could hear the dogs running and the faint jingle of the leaders' bells. As she left the enclosure and secured the gate, Tumble and Max burst into sight. "They're coming awfully fast."

She and her mother stepped back as the team tore into the yard. Robyn backed up against the fence, debating whether to interfere.

"Whoa." Grandpa was riding the brake, but the dogs were still pulling too hard.

A shot of adrenaline hit Robyn. They took the curve in the pathway too fast, and the sled swung around on one runner. Usually by this time of year, the snow was deeper and the sides of the trail banked, but now the sled weaved all over the place. Grandpa wasn't heavy enough to slow the breakneck pace.

The young dogs used the near wreck as an excuse to leap in excitement, and the older, steadier leaders seemed to catch their mood.

"Tumble!" Robyn stepped forward. "Whoa, Max!" They raced past her with the sled swaying so wildly Robyn had to jump out of the way.

Grandpa's mouth hung open, and he looked ahead, judging the stopping distance needed before they would crash into the shed that held dog food and tools.

"Dad!" her mother yelled.

Robyn took off in a sprint. If she could jump on the runner beside Grandpa, that might slow them down enough.

"Whoa, you numbskulls!" Grandpa clutched the handlebar and braced for the impact. The sled swung around before Robyn could reach it and hit the corner of the wall.

Max and Tumble swerved at the last second, dragging the young dogs with them. The wheelers took the weight of the sled as they tried to turn and avoid the shed, but Coco slammed into it with her right shoulder. She yelped in pain as the sled slid sideways and tipped over, dumping Grandpa to the ground.

Robyn ran forward. "Grandpa! Are you hurt?"

Grandpa Steve raised his head and looked after the team that still ran, pulling the damaged sled. "Get the dogs! The dogs, Robby! Don't let them run free."

He was right, of course. Robyn ran after the sled, calling to the leaders and reasoning to herself that if he were seriously hurt, he wouldn't have yelled at her like that. Her job was to make sure they stopped running before they got to the highway.

She called to the leaders again. At last Max turned them, just before they reached the road. They made a wide arc into the unbroken snow, and it slowed the dogs down. They came back toward her, panting and wagging their tails. The two youngsters still danced in their harness. The sled skidded along behind them on its side. Coco limped, and her harness mate, Rocky, seemed to have his outside hind leg tangled in the lines.

Robyn spoke sternly to the leaders, and they lay down, eyeing her sheepishly. The wheelers followed, and after a moment the dogs in the middle slunk down and put their chins on their paws.

Robyn took several deep breaths. They were dogs. They were trained to run and to love pulling the sled. It wasn't really their fault.

It was her fault.

She'd known deep down that Grandpa couldn't handle a team of fresh dogs anymore. He'd once been a strong man, but those days were over. Between the weight he'd lost in the last year and the muscle he'd lost through lack of exercise, he never should have attempted the stunt. And she should have stopped him.

She unhooked the sled and left it beside the driveway, gathering the end of the towline firmly. "Hike." Grimly, she walked behind the eight dogs. More subdued now, they obeyed and headed back toward the dog lot, where their individual doghouses sat.

To her surprise, Grandpa still lay on the ground near the shed. Her mother knelt beside him in the snow.

"Is he okay?" Robyn called.

"We're taking it slow and easy," Mom replied. The look she threw Robyn did nothing to allay her fears.

Robyn tied the team up with a snub line and hurried to Grandpa's side.

"They got away from me," he said ruefully. "I just couldn't hold 'em."

"Well, Dad, don't fret about it. We need to take you to the ER and make sure you didn't do any serious damage."

"Naw, I don't need to go to any hospital."

"I'll make the rest of the decisions today, thank you." Robyn's mother stood and arched her eyebrows. "Can you help me get him up?"

"Is it serious?" Robyn asked.

"I don't think anything's broken, but he bumped his head on the sled and landed pretty hard on his hip."

Robyn lowered her voice. "You're taking him in?"

Her mother hesitated. "If he can walk, we'll take him inside and let him rest. If not, we'll get him to the car and head for the hospital."

"Now, Cheryl," Grandpa protested through clenched teeth, "all I need is a heating pad."

"We'll see." She knelt again beside him.

Robyn got on his other side and slid her arm under his head, around his shoulders. "You ready, Grandpa?"

He strained to sit up but quickly lay back with a moan. After a moment, he said, "Let me roll over on my side. It'll be easier that way."

Gently, she rolled him over. He seized her wrist. With both women lifting, he got to his feet with a groan. "Oh man, that hurts."

"Can you put weight on it?" Mom asked.

"I'm not sure."

"Robyn, honey, go bring my car around here."

"I'll drive," Robyn said.

"No, you stay and put the dogs away. And call the store. Tell them I won't be in this morning."

Robyn dashed around front and brought the car to the dog lot. By the time she got there, Grandpa sagged heavily against her mom, his face contorted in pain. They got him into the backseat, and her mother drove away, her mouth set in a grim line.

Robyn walked slowly to where she'd tied up the team. "Made a real mess, didn't you all? That will teach us to put two rookies in the team at once. Shouldn't have rushed it."

But she knew the accident hadn't happened because of the yearlings. She'd run half-grown pups with her team many times in training. That was how they learned. And each had been harnessed alongside an older, calmer dog. No, it was Grandpa's refusal to face the reality of his condition, and her reluctance to force him to admit it.

She felt Coco's leg. "You all right, girl?"

Coco licked her hand.

"I know it wasn't your fault." Robyn reached into her pocket for a treat and slipped it into Coco's mouth. Her hands shook as she unhooked the dogs one by one, led them to their kennels, and removed their harnesses. All the time she berated herself. They couldn't afford mistakes like that. How badly was Grandpa injured? Would Medicare pay for his treatment? The sled would need repair. She'd have to back up several steps in the new dogs' training. How many slow, steady runs would it take to undo what happened today? How long before they knew they were no longer in control?

She would have to proceed cautiously, to make sure she stayed in control and the dogs never tasted that freedom again. Her mind raced, thinking of ways to set things up so that today's fiasco never occurred again. Some extra weight on the sled next time would be a start. And she wouldn't run this particular group of dogs together again for a while. She'd take one or two of this batch at a time, mixing them with others who hadn't taken part in the episode.

She went into the house and filled two buckets of water. As the water ran, she remembered to call her mother's supervisor at the store. She cleaned out the dogs' dishes, surprised that the ice hadn't melted yet. It seemed like hours since she'd brought the dishes in. Most of them had thawed enough that the thick circles of ice fell out when she tipped the dishes up in the sink.

She carried the water to the dogs then dragged the sled up near the barn. She might be able to fix the wooden frame.

An hour later she still bent over it, almost finished, when her phone rang. She fumbled in her pocket for it. "Mom?"

"Yeah. They're doing a CT scan, but the doctor wants to keep Grandpa here overnight regardless of the results."

Robyn exhaled and fought back hot, painful tears. "Mom, I'm sorry."

"What for? It wasn't your fault."

Robyn swiped at her eyes with her free hand and sniffed. "I never should have let Grandpa drive. What was I thinking?"

"Oh, as if you could stop him."

"I know, but—"

"Honey, listen to me. We both know he's grown frailer over the last few years. He's done better this summer and fall, but he's still not strong. The trouble is, he's independent, too. He doesn't want to think he's too old to ever mush again. And neither one of us wanted to tell him the truth, because we love him."

Robyn pulled in a deep breath, knowing her mom talked

sense. "If the dogs had a mind to, they could have been in Palmer in an hour. At least Max and Tumble turned the team around and came back."

"Yes, thank the Lord. They brought the team back safe. But it's time Dad stopped mushing, just like it was time he quit driving the truck."

Robyn swallowed hard. "I don't like to think of it. He's loved sledding all his life. And he's taught me so much!"

"I know, honey. But this is the way it's got to be. Now, if you're okay, I'm going to call the store and see if they can use me for a few hours. We can come in together and see Grandpa tonight."

"Okay." Robyn knew they needed the money. Mom couldn't afford to miss her part-time job if she didn't have to.

She put her phone away and went back to work on the sled. Grandpa made this sled, and it was a good one. He was never far from her thoughts as she worked. Without his mentoring, she'd never have learned as much about dogs as she did. She certainly wouldn't have had the opportunity to go into dog breeding and training as a business.

But today she felt like Alaska's biggest failure.

❧

The next morning, Robyn rose at her usual time—five o'clock—and began preparing the dogs' breakfasts. Though Grandpa usually got up an hour later nowadays, she missed him, knowing he wouldn't be around today. The knowledge that he wouldn't eat breakfast with her after she'd fed the dogs saddened her.

"There've been a lot of changes in the last few years," Grandpa used to say, "and I've been against all of them."

Robyn pushed up the sleeves of her hoodie and sniffed. She could do without any more changes herself. First her older brother, Aven, had joined the Coast Guard. Then their father had died three years ago. Now she'd lost Grandpa, too, at least temporarily. Would it be just her and Mom from now on?

She opened the refrigerator for the meat she'd put in there to thaw overnight. Some people fed commercial food, but the dogs performed better if they ate mostly meat, so that's what the Hollands fed. Grandpa Steve had experimented over the years with several different feeding programs, and he'd worked out his own formula for a summer diet, changing to one with more fat and certain other nutrients as the racing season approached.

Since his arthritis had worsened, Robyn did most of the heavy work. Grandpa still played a big role in training teams for serious mushers and tending the dogs they raised to sell. He loved playing with the puppies, too.

"Hey, honey. Need any help?"

Robyn turned in surprise to see her mother, eyes puffy from sleep, standing in the doorway.

"No, I'm fine, Mom. Go back to bed."

"Figured I'd help you this morning and then run to the hospital to see Grandpa before work." On Wednesday afternoons, Cheryl put in four hours at the grocery store on the highway.

"I'll be okay." Robyn flashed a smile she didn't feel.

"Well, be careful if you do a training run."

"I will." She was always careful; but then, accidents had a way of catching you unaware. She hefted two buckets of dog feed and carried them toward the back door. "If Coco's still limping, I'll call Rick Baker to see if he can look at her. And maybe I'll call Darby later and see if she can come play with the puppies for a while."

Her mother sprang forward to open the door for her, so Robyn wouldn't have to set the buckets down. "She'd probably love to, and I'll feel better if I know you're not all alone here."

"Mom, don't let Grandpa's accident worry you too much. He's going to be okay."

"I don't like his head injury. That CT scan they did

yesterday showed a little bleeding in his brain. That's not good. I'll feel better when the doctor says he's going to be all right."

❧

Rick Baker was headed out the door with his medical bag when his phone rang. He paused in the kitchen and answered it.

"Hi, Dr. Baker? Rick? It's Robyn."

He smiled at her tentative greeting. "Yes, it's me, Robyn. Is anything wrong?" The pretty young woman next door rarely called him, and if she did, it usually meant her dogs needed his professional care. Sometimes he wished she wanted to see him because he was Rick, not because he was the vet who lived close by. He'd been too busy, though, to pursue the idea or the woman.

"One of my dogs had an accident yesterday. Actually, eight of them did, but Coco seems to be the only one who's hurt. She and Grandpa."

"Your grandfather was injured?"

"Yes." Her voice drooped like a slack towline. "He's at the hospital."

"What happened?"

She hesitated. "It's my fault. I let him take a team out. He thought he could handle them. I tried to tell him they were too much for him, but he wanted to do it so badly. I. . .I caved."

Rick could almost see her mournful dark eyes. He knew she was well past twenty years old, but today she sounded like a frightened kid.

"Is it serious?"

"We're not sure yet. They did some tests yesterday, and they're going to do a few more today. Mom's there now."

He glanced at his watch. If he stopped at the Hollands', he'd arrive at the clinic a few minutes late. But Robyn sounded like she needed a little reassurance. "Would you like me to take a look at Coco before I head for Anchorage?"

"Oh, today's your day at the clinic, isn't it?"

"Actually, I'm doing two days a week now. But I can take a quick look."

"I'd really appreciate it."

Ten minutes later he walked across the Hollands' dog lot with Robyn. She described the runaway sled and showed him where the team had collided with the shed wall. She took him into the female dogs' enclosure and led him to Coco's tether.

He stooped to greet the injured husky. "Hey there, Coco." He let the dog sniff his hands before touching her. "Where does it hurt, girl?"

"She hit her right front leg hardest." Robyn squatted beside him. "She's probably sore all over today."

Rick took his gloves off and ran his hand over the dog's shoulder and leg. "It's a little warm, and there seems to be some swelling. Not broken, though."

She nodded. "So, rest? What else?"

"Did she eat her breakfast?"

"Yeah."

He checked the dog's eyes and general appearance. Coco seemed alert and happy to see him. He felt her pulse and watched her respiration for a moment. "Okay. Give her a couple of days off, and make sure she keeps warm." He glanced toward the doghouse. The Hollands were good about providing shelter and bedding for their dogs in winter. "If she seems better then, start light exercise. Let her run free if you can, or put her on a leash and walk her around for ten or fifteen minutes. If she's no worse the next day, do a little more. . . . And I'll try to stop in again tomorrow and see how she's doing."

"Thanks."

He stood and pulled his gloves on. "No problem. And if she's worse, give me a call." They walked toward the gate. "I hope your grandfather's all right."

"Mom will probably come back for lunch before she goes to work. She'll tell me what the doctor said then."

Robyn looked young and vulnerable in her blue quilted jacket. Her dark hair hung in a thick braid over her shoulder, and her eyes held self-reproach.

"Hey." He reached out with his gloved hand and tilted her chin up. "You're not blaming yourself for your granddad's accident, are you?"

She shrugged. "I shouldn't have let him take the team out."

Rick considered that. Steve Holland was a stubborn old man. He'd forgotten more about dogs than most men ever learned, and he could dig in his heels when he wanted to.

"Who does your mother blame?" he asked.

Robyn hesitated a moment and looked down. "Grandpa."

"And who does Grandpa blame?"

"Himself."

Rick nodded. "So tell me, who's blaming Robyn?"

She smiled sheepishly but said nothing.

"Right. We all know you couldn't have stopped him, don't we?" Before she could protest, he turned her chin again, so that she looked up into his eyes. "This is not your fault."

"Okay." She held his gaze, and Rick took his time soaking in the view. He'd known Robyn a little over a year, and she intrigued him. She had a toughness the Alaska terrain and family hardships had taught her, but she had a tender side, too—the one that made her feel guilty when she didn't deserve it. She stirred a protectiveness in him, but he sensed she wouldn't accept that from a man unless she was desperate. Or in love.

"I'm going to call you tonight," he said on impulse.

Her eyebrows rose, forming delicate arches.

He nodded. "I want to check on Coco and your grandpa. So be ready with a report this evening."

She smiled. "That's nice of you. Thanks."

"No trouble." He left her and walked out toward his pickup. Fifteen minutes late, but fifteen minutes well spent. And tonight when he called, it would be as much to gauge Robyn's spirits as to check on the two patients. He looked forward to it, and he hadn't even left her driveway yet.

two

At about eleven o'clock, Robyn heard her mother drive in. When she went into the house, her mom was just ending a phone conversation.

"Hi, honey. That was a potential customer. A man from California is interested in buying some dogs."

"That's great," Robyn said. "It would be good to sell a few yearlings. That would help our cash flow and give us more space for boarders."

"Yeah. He. . .wants to buy some breeding stock. He's coming next week to look over what you have."

Robyn stared at her. "I don't want to sell my breeding stock, Mom. You know that."

"Honey, we may not have a choice. Besides, you've got some adult dogs you planned on selling, haven't you?"

"A few." Robyn washed her hands at the sink. Since Dad died, they'd gotten by with the dog business and her mother's part-time job. But Mom worried a lot about their finances. She never seemed to believe they would have enough money to pay the bills each month. Sometimes Robyn thought Mom would rather get rid of all the dogs and live a "normal" life. But Robyn couldn't live without dogs.

She picked up the towel and dried her hands. "How's Grandpa?"

"Not so good. His bruises look terrible today." Mom shook her head and sighed. "It's his head injury that's got the doctor worried though. He's concerned enough that he wants to monitor Grandpa for another day or two."

"Well. . ." Robyn eyed her cautiously. "I guess that's best for him."

"Yes, I'm sure it is. It could get expensive, though."

"Won't Medicare pay for it?"

"For the hospital stay, yes, if it's not too long. But his muscles won't be used to working when he's ready to leave the hospital. The doctor said they'll probably transfer him to a skilled care nursing home for a couple of weeks of rehab."

Robyn let that sink in. No wonder her mother hadn't discouraged the dog buyer.

"I don't want to sell my breeding dogs, Mom. Or my leaders. I need them for training."

Her mother nodded but said nothing. They finished eating in silence.

❧

Darby Zale arrived at the Hollands' home soon after the school bus passed.

Robyn called to her and let her in to wait while she pulled on her jacket, boots, and gloves.

At sixteen, Darby hovered between exuberant kid and gorgeous woman. Her thick auburn hair and flawless skin frequently motivated Robyn to pray that she wouldn't be envious. It wasn't fair for a girl as young as Darby to look so good without even trying.

Darkness had already fallen, and Robyn put on her headlamp and handed Darby a flashlight before they went out the back door.

"They're getting so big!" Darby sidled through the gate with Robyn, into the puppy enclosure at one side of the dog yard.

"Yeah, they're getting pretty good at taking a few commands. It's time to start putting the puppy harness on them."

"Oh, I love it when we do that."

Robyn nodded. "Okay. I've got six dogs I want to take out for a training run. Why don't you play with the pups while I do that, and afterward, we'll do a short session with them."

"Great!" Darby gladly hung about the Hollands' kennels

to help with the dogs and learn about sledding and training. Robyn got the team's harnesses ready and coached Darby through slipping one onto Rounder, an energetic three-year-old she hoped to sell soon. If the potential customer wanted fast, strong sled dogs and didn't care about breeding. . .she refused to think about it for the moment.

She handed Darby another harness. They hitched up the rest of the team she would exercise—several veterans and one yearling. Robyn hooked the towline to the repaired sled and waved to Darby, who stood near the puppy pen.

Getting out onto the trail always made Robyn feel more alive. She didn't mind sledding in the dark, though it hid the valley's magnificent scenery from her. You had to get used to it, or you wouldn't get much training time in Wasilla. This time of year, the area got only about four hours of daylight, and the air temperatures generally stayed below freezing. The dogs loved it.

She belonged out here, too. The crisp, fresh air and the firm snow perked her up and made her want to ride on and on. The dogs pulled eagerly beneath the moon. Her initial concerns about the sled she'd repaired seemed unfounded—it moved just as it should and held together.

She swung behind Rick Baker's house. The veterinarian had assured her that she could take the dogs over his property any time, and Robyn liked having some different scenery for the dogs. Rick's land also held a short section of the 100-mile trail for the Fire & Ice, the annual race the Holland Kennel sponsored in January. Several other landowners let them run over their property and turned out to help man checkpoints for the race.

As the dogs pulled her along, she prayed silently for Grandpa. If he went to the rehab place, would he be able to come home in time for this year's race? They'd received forty-eight entries—a record number for the Fire & Ice. Some of the names on the list impressed even Grandpa, who knew every musher in Alaska. A few well-known dog racers liked to use the Hollands' race as a warm-up for longer competitions or a training ground for young dogs. That suited Robyn just fine. It gave the Hollands an opportunity to display their kennel and dogs they had raised to potential customers.

The race fell on January twenty-third this year, which gave her only a few weeks to complete all the preparations. Without Grandpa's help, she would carry most of the load.

When she got back to the house half an hour later, Darby came smiling from the puppies' enclosure. "How'd they do?" she called.

"Perfect." Robyn stopped the team and started to set the snow hook. "Hey, do you know how to use one of these?"

"Not very well," Darby admitted, eyeing the metal hook uncertainly.

"Well, come on, girl. Now that we've got plenty of snow again, it's time you learned." Robyn beckoned her over and showed her how to push the hook into the snow near the sled, so that she could step on it and anchor it well while holding onto the sled's handlebar. She had the dogs move forward a little, putting tension on the anchor line.

"Now, if you want to release it, they have to back up." She pulled back on the sled, and the dogs inched backward. "As long as they're pulling on the line, if you've set it right, they can't go."

"That is so cool. Can I try it?"

Robyn grinned. "When you can do it right, I'll let you mush around the yard."

Darby was an apt pupil, and in less than ten minutes Robyn unhooked the two youngest dogs from the towline and rearranged the four older dogs.

"Okay. Don't forget to hold onto the sled when you take the snow hook off. If you can stand on the brake with one foot while you do it, that's even better." Robyn stood near the leaders, just in case. She didn't want another runaway team.

Darby pulled on the rope attached to the top of the hook and released it without trouble. The dogs twitched when they heard it come out of the snow.

"Brake," Robyn called.

Darby quickly put all her weight on the brake board.

"You're good," Robyn assured her. "Now wind up the rope and stow the hook. You don't want it dragging along behind the sled."

Darby fumbled with the line. "I'm nervous."

"Take your time. The dogs will know you're antsy, and they will be, too." Robyn was glad she'd cut the team down to four dogs. She'd considered letting Darby take them outside the enclosure today, but thought better of it. With a little more practice, Darby would gain the confidence she needed to control the team without the aid of a fence. For now, a trot around the path inside the yard would be enough.

After Darby's short ride, they put the dogs and the harness away and spent some time with the puppies, putting the small harness on each one for just a few minutes. Robyn was pleased that most of them obeyed her "sit" and "come" commands without error.

"Guess I'd better get home." Darby looked toward the sky. The moon still hung overhead.

"Thanks for the help," Robyn said. "Do you want me to drive you home in the truck?"

"No, I'll be okay if I leave now."

"Take the flashlight."

"Thanks. Can I come back tomorrow?"

"Yes. Oh—call first. I'm not sure if Grandpa's coming home or not."

"I hope he will. Bye." Darby dashed down the driveway.

Robyn went into the house and filled the woodstove. She liked to have a hot supper waiting when her mother got home from work. Afterward, she would feed the dogs with the aid of the lights in the dog lot and a powerful flashlight. Half the year at least she did her chores after dark or before the sun rose. She'd never lived anywhere else, so she expected it. But Aven had told her he'd had trouble sleeping when he went for his Coast Guard training in New Jersey. The sun never seemed to rise or set at the right time. After that, he'd served for a while in the Gulf of Mexico, and between the lack of snow and the comparatively long daylight hours in winter, he'd felt displaced at first.

"I kind of liked it after a while," he'd confessed to her. "It was too hot in summer, but the rest of the year was nice. I don't think people got as depressed as they do up here in the winter."

She puttered about the kitchen, thinking over what her mother had told her at noon. Grandpa's medical care could place a financial burden on them. He didn't have a large amount of savings. Most of what they all earned went for family expenses and maintaining the dogs and equipment. They'd each received a payment in the fall from Alaska's Permanent Fund, and right now they were solvent. But that would only go so far.

Robyn's biggest income came from selling puppies and older dogs she and Grandpa had trained. Sometimes she trained dogs for other people, but most serious mushers trained their own dogs. Right now she had a team of eight belonging to a sledder who had suffered appendicitis and undergone surgery. He'd asked her to take some of his dogs for six weeks and keep them in shape, so he wouldn't lose ground on training for the upcoming races. The other forty dogs out back were Holland dogs. Their upkeep was a spendy enterprise.

Mom came home about six o'clock with the trunk of her car full of groceries.

Robyn couldn't help noticing the fatigue lines at the corners of her eyes as she helped unload. "Are you going to the hospital tonight?" she asked.

"No, I don't think so. I called the nurses' station before I left work. Grandpa's doing all right and resting. I told her we'd come in the morning. I don't have to work tomorrow, and I thought you'd like to see him."

"Yes, I would."

Her mother nodded. "The doctor might know for sure by then what they plan to do to continue treatment."

"If they move him to a nursing home, will it be in Anchorage?" Robyn asked.

"I'm not sure yet. Guess we'll have to do some research."

"Maybe I can get online later."

Her mother smiled wearily. "That would be good. Would you like help feeding tonight?"

"I can do it," Robyn said, though she'd have been glad for an extra pair of hands. Her mother looked wrung out.

"Okay, then I'm going to pack a few things to take to Dad tomorrow. He wants his razor and his Bible. I'll take some clean clothes, too, in case they release him."

Robyn took out her cell phone and checked it before she went out to feed the dogs. They'd given up the land line to save money the year before and relied on their cells now. She hoped Rick would remember his promise to call her.

❧

"Hey, Rick, any chance you can cover for me next Monday?" Bob Major, the principal partner of the Far North Veterinary Hospital in Anchorage, stopped him in the lobby before Rick could get out the door.

"Uh. . ." Rick quickly tabulated all the things on his agenda for Monday. "I don't think so, Bob. I've got a lot of patient visits lined up in the Palmer area and office hours in Wasilla. Besides, you already said you need me next Thursday."

Major shrugged. "It was worth a try. I'll have to rearrange my schedule is all. Or have Lucy rearrange it." He looked toward the receptionist's desk and winked at her.

Lucy, who had worked for Bob and his partner, Hap Shelley, for several years, rolled her eyes. "What else is new?"

Bob laughed. "I'll see you Friday."

"On call only, right? We're officially closed for New Year's, Hap told me."

"True, but we've got some inpatients you'll need to treat, and there are always a few emergency calls."

"Right. I'll be here." Rick nodded at Lucy and escaped. The drive home to Wasilla would take a good forty-five minutes. He disliked the commute, which would probably get harder as winter went on. Why had he ever agreed to do two days a week in Anchorage? He'd left full-time practice with Far North a year ago, but the other two doctors insisted they still needed him to man the clinic some of the time. Rick had agreed to continue working one day a week in Anchorage and opened his small veterinary practice in Wasilla. He'd reasoned that he might not have enough business to support him up there and should keep the ties to the larger practice strong in case his new venture didn't work out.

Talk about underestimation. Despite the fact that several other veterinarians worked in the area, he'd soon found that he couldn't handle all the business waiting for him in the Mat-Su Valley if he'd cloned himself. But Bob had pleaded with him a month ago to add a second day to his weekly commitment at the Anchorage clinic. Rick had reluctantly agreed. Now Bob wanted him to cover on extra days.

Rick slid behind the wheel of his pickup, thankful he'd had the courage to refuse. The way things were going, they'd soon try to draw him back into the Anchorage practice full time. Bob and Hap had already hinted that they'd started looking for a new partner to replace Bob when he retired. It would be a secure position for Rick, and a better income. He could move back to Anchorage and not have to drive so far. In the city, most of the patients came to him. In the valley, he made as many house calls as office visits. And he wouldn't be risking his life savings on a new venture.

But every time he drove to the city, Rick found himself a little more certain he didn't want to do that. He loved his log home on the outskirts of Wasilla. The building he rented in town for his practice wasn't ideal, but it was adequate. He hoped one day to build a spacious new facility, where he could provide complete services, within a few miles of Iditarod Headquarters. Maybe he'd be the one bringing in a partner. It was a big dream, but at thirty-three, Rick knew what he wanted. His own practice. His own home. Someday, his own family.

He used the first part of the drive to pray for his patients and his work situation then popped in a CD. By the time he reached his driveway, the tension was gone. A slight pang of regret nudged him as he unlocked the door to the empty house. It would be nice to have someone waiting for him. But with his long days on the road, he didn't feel he could have even a dog at home. He wouldn't like to neglect one, and he couldn't see taking one with him to the clinic. Too complicated.

The house was cold. He ran the heat low while he was away from home. A fire in the woodstove tonight might be enough to keep him warm. He'd heard temperatures would fall later in the week, though, to zero or below. He'd have to rely more on the furnace.

After he'd gotten the place warmed up and fixed dinner in the microwave, he remembered he'd promised to call Robyn.

She sounded a little breathless when she answered.

"Hi," Rick said. "Everything okay over there?"

"Yes, thanks. Coco seemed a little better tonight. I rubbed her shoulder for a few minutes when I fed her."

"Good. How's Mr. Holland?"

"Well. . .they're keeping him tonight and maybe tomorrow. But Mom says the doctor will probably recommend rehabilitation after that. Instead of sending him home, they may put him in a skilled care home for a little while."

"That may be what's best for him right now," Rick said. "I know it's hard to face, but if he needs therapy, let the professionals help him. Chances are he'll feel better and be able to do more when he finally comes home than he did before the accident."

"Maybe." She sighed. "I've been praying all day. I know Grandpa would hate having to go somewhere else. He doesn't like being away from home anyway, and being in the city would be a double blow for him. Mom thinks the rehab place would be in Anchorage."

"That's rough," Rick said. "I hate to think of you and your mom having to go back and forth a lot. If it's any help, I'd be happy to give either of you a ride when I'm going that way."

"Thanks a lot."

He wished he could put a smile in her voice. Robyn usually presented a sunny attitude. What would cheer her up? One thing came to mind. "Hey, I was asked today if I'd help oversee the 'dropped dog' station for the Iditarod in March."

"Oh, that is so cool. I'd love to get that assignment."

"You want to help? I can try to get your name on the list of volunteers."

"Really?" She hesitated. "We always do something during the Iditarod, usually here in the valley. But it would be great to help tend the dogs during the race."

"Yeah. I always feel bad for mushers who have to drop a dog, but they do get tired or injured sometimes. We'll give them the best care when they're flown to Anchorage, until their owners can pick them up again."

"Let me talk to Mom about it, okay? If she wants to help at one of the checkpoints up here, I should probably stay with her."

"Just let me know. Can't guarantee you a spot, but I'll use what influence I'll have as a team leader."

"Thanks."

She sounded happier now, and Rick hated to end the conversation. Tomorrow was New Year's Eve, and there'd be a celebration downtown. Should he ask her? People would be out watching the Northern Lights and generally raising a riot. He'd planned to avoid the noisy gathering. Besides, did he really want to stay up that late after a full day making his rounds? He decided not. "Well, I'll stop in tomorrow and take a look at Coco."

"Good. Oh, I plan to go with Mom around ten in the morning to see Grandpa."

"I'll come earlier. Eight all right?"

"Perfect."

"Robyn, if you need help with anything, let me know."

"Thanks, I will. I know you're busy."

"Hey, I mean it. And I plan to help out at your race this year, too."

"Oh, good. I was hoping you would. I tentatively put you down for pre-race vet checks, and we'll have you evaluate the dogs when they finish, too, if you can do it."

"Fantastic. I love the way all the people in town help out on race day."

"Me, too," she said. "Only three weeks to go. My friend Anna is keeping track of the volunteers, and she said nearly all the spots are filled. It's always a blessing to see the people come out and help us."

Rick signed off and settled in his recliner with a book, but his thoughts kept drifting back to Robyn and their conversation. It reaffirmed his decision about Far North Veterinary. They could find another vet. His place was here in Wasilla now.

❧

"Why can't I just go home?" Grandpa Steve folded his arms across his chest and glared up at his doctor.

"I don't think you're ready just yet," Dr. Mellin said with a smile. She shone her flashlight into Grandpa's eyes, observing with a frown. "A couple of weeks at rehab will do a lot for you. It'll give you a chance to regain your strength and balance. We don't want you to go home and have a fall and wind up back in here."

Robyn glanced at her mother. Leave it to Grandpa to kick up a fuss, but then, she'd expected that.

"Isn't there a place here in Wasilla?" Mom asked.

Dr. Mellin straightened and shook her head. "I'm afraid not. Will it be a hardship for you if he goes to Anchorage?"

Mom shrugged. "Some, but we'll do whatever we have to. Won't we, Dad?"

He snorted and refused to meet her gaze.

"Grandpa," Robyn said, "you've got to do what the doctor says. When you get better, then we'll bring you home."

"People go into nursing homes and don't come out."

Robyn almost laughed at his passionate scowl, but something in her stomach twisted. He mirrored her fear exactly, down to the childish expression.

"Mr. Holland, I'm only recommending this because I think it's the best course of treatment for you. We can't keep you here more than another day, given your condition."

"What does that mean?" His eyebrows pulled together as he looked up at her.

"It means you're getting better, but you're not completely well. Your head injury seems to be healing, and in a few days your bruises will go away. But your muscles need some attention. Let us get you the treatment you need and send you home in a couple of weeks in good shape."

"A couple of weeks? You hear that, Cheryl? I can't come home for two weeks."

"That's my estimate based on what I see today." Dr. Mellin consulted the chart. "If you behave yourself, that ought to do it. No guarantees though. So. . .I'll refer you, and if nothing's changed for the worse, we'll release you tomorrow."

Mom stood. "How will he get to the rehab place?"

"He doesn't really need an ambulance. If you are able to drive him to Anchorage, it would save the expense. I think he'll ride fine in a private car for that distance."

"Mom, I can take him," Robyn said. "You have to work tomorrow afternoon."

"I could take the day off. I think I'd like to take him myself, honey." Mom smiled at her. "No offense, and if you want to come along, that's fine. I just want to be there to help him get settled."

"Will I be able wear my own clothes?" Grandpa threw back the covers. "These johnnies are worthless. I want my pajamas."

Dr. Mellin smiled. "I think they'll let you wear pajamas, sir. And now you should rest. I'll pop in this evening to see what you're up to. Don't run the nurses ragged today, you hear?"

"Who. . .me?"

Mom peeled back the blanket and replaced the sheet over Grandpa's thin legs. "Dad, she's kidding."

"Ha."

Dr. Mellin laughed and headed for the door. "See you later, Mr. Holland."

"After awhile, crocodile." He frowned up at his daughter-in-law. "Cheryl, they don't know how to make apple crisp here."

"Relax. I brought you some cookies."

"What about my razor?"

"Yes. Do you want to shave?" Mom asked.

"Not now. What kind of cookies?"

Robyn pulled the plastic container from her tote bag and sat down on the edge of his bed. "Gingersnaps and peanut butter. Mom had a bake-fest last night. Which do you want first?"

"Ginger snaps." He looked around at the nightstand and spotted a glass of water with a straw in it. "Can you reach my drink?"

Robyn handed it to him.

After the first cookie, Grandpa switched to peanut butter. "How's Coco doing?" he asked.

"She's okay. Dr. Baker looked at her yesterday and again this morning. He thinks she'll be fine."

Grandpa's eyebrows shot up. "Rick made two house calls?"

"Well. . .yes, if you want to get technical."

"Are we paying him for it?"

"I. . ." Robyn looked around helplessly at her mother.

"I think Rick stopped in as a neighbor, Dad. Don't worry about it."

"But if he's doing vet stuff, we should pay him."

"I'll make a point of asking him to send us a bill," Mom said.

Grandpa sighed and lay back on his pillows. "I made a big mess, didn't I? I bet my vet bills are going to be a lot more than Coco's."

His eyelids drifted shut, and Robyn glanced at her mother. They'd stopped at the billing office on the way in. Most of this hospital stay would be covered, but they'd learned only seven days of Grandpa's rehab would be paid for. If he stayed in treatment longer than that, the family would be expected to pay for it.

Mom had leaned back in her chair and closed her eyes. She looked exhausted. Robyn determined to ask Darby to help her feed in the morning. She needed to be finished early—in time to go with Mom when she moved Grandpa to Anchorage.

three

Darkness had fallen when they returned to the house the next afternoon. Robyn was surprised to see Rick's pickup in the yard when she drove in.

He ambled around the corner of the house from the direction of the dog lot as she parked. "Hi," he called. "Need any help?"

"No, thanks," Mom said. "We don't have much to carry."

"How's Steve?"

"All settled at the nursing home."

"That's good. I hope he does well there." Rick looked at Robyn. "Hope you don't mind, I went out back and looked at Coco. She seems to have recovered well."

"I think so, too. I asked Darby to take her out on the leash for a few minutes this morning. I'll be around tomorrow to work all these lazy dogs."

Rick smiled and walked with her as she followed Mom into the house. "It's a big job, getting them all in shape. Especially in this cold weather."

"Yes. And I have several I hope to sell. They need to be in top condition when the buyers start looking."

"When will that be?"

Robyn stopped in the living room and faced him. Mom was in the kitchen, out of earshot. "Actually, we have someone coming next week to look at a few of the dogs."

"You don't sound too happy about that."

She took a breath and looked away. "I'm not. He wants breeding stock, and those aren't the dogs I want to sell right now. But. . .I may not have a choice."

"Everything all right?" Quickly he added, "I don't mean to

33

pry, but if there's anything I can help with. . ."

"Things are a little tight financially. But hey, they always are around here." She pulled out a smile for him.

"I've been praying for your family."

His simple statement comforted her. She'd picked up on a few things he'd said in the past, but he'd never come to the little church her family attended in Wasilla. Grandpa had a bolder nature than she did though. He'd pinned Rick down verbally once while he was examining a new litter of puppies. Robyn wished she'd been there. Grandpa had told her later that Rick shared their faith. Actually, Grandpa's exact words were, "Just what we need. A vet who knows his Bible *and* his medical books."

"Thank you. Pray that we'll have what's needed for Grandpa's care, and that he'll be ready to come home soon, so we don't have to pay too much."

"How long will he need physical therapy?"

"The doctor estimated two weeks—which is more than he's covered for."

Rick nodded. "Got it. I'll be praying about the race, too. It's not that far away, and I know your grandfather usually helps a lot with that."

"Three weeks." Robyn caught her lower lip between her teeth.

"Are you nervous about it?"

"Yeah. I'm not sure how we'll do. There's a meeting next Saturday for all the volunteers. If you're busy, it's okay."

"I'll be there. What time?"

"Ten o'clock, at Iditarod Headquarters. They're letting us use the meeting room."

"Nice."

She nodded. "Mom is helping a lot, but it's been tough since my dad died. Grandpa and I do most of the race preparation, and we get friends to help. My brother and his wife plan to come the week of the race. Aven's terrific. He'll do all the last-minute heavy work. Ormand Lesley is our race marshal. He does a lot of work, too. And we've got people organizing the mushers' drop bags and communications and—oh, a thousand other things."

"Even a race of this scale is a ton of work, isn't it?"

"It sure is. But we've done whatever we had to in order to keep it going these last few years. The success of the Fire & Ice is important to our business."

"I thought it might be. I'm happy to volunteer my services for the day."

"I'll give you the toughest duties."

He grinned. "That's what I want. Let me at it. And if the route will allow me to do the check-in exams and then go off to another spot farther down the line, I'll do it. I know the teams loop around and come back to the start, but I might be able to help someplace else for a few hours. Whatever you need."

"That's terrific. I'll take you up on it." She stood for a moment, looking up into his gleaming eyes. Rick Baker could surely give a girl ideas.

"Hey, let me help you feed the dogs tonight," he said.

"Really? You don't need to."

"I know. I want to. You've been gone all day, and I'll bet you're tired."

"Okay, you asked for it. I've got meat in the refrigerator. The rest of it's out in the barn."

She led him into the kitchen. Mom bent over a base cabinet and pulled out a frying pan. "Feel like a grilled cheese sandwich, Robyn?"

"Sure. Thanks. Dr. Baker's going to help me feed the mutts, so it won't take long."

"Rick, have you had supper?" Mom asked. "It's not fancy, but I can make a few extra sandwiches without any trouble."

"Well. . ." He eyed her with his eyebrows arched.

"Why not?" Robyn asked. "You'll be earning your keep."

He laughed. "All right. Thank you, Mrs. Holland."

"It's Cheryl. And thank *you*. I think Robyn and I are both frazzled tonight."

A note was tacked to the door of the shed they referred to as the "the barn."

> Happy New Year! I cuddled the puppies for a bit and cleaned out their pen. See you tomorrow.
>
> Darby

Rick read it over her shoulder. "She's a good kid," he said.

"Yes. She loves dogs, and she's a big help to me lately. I wish I could afford to pay her."

"She's getting paid in the knowledge you're giving her."

Robyn nodded. "I promised her I'd teach her to drive the sled this winter. She's had a couple of lessons. She'll be good at it."

In less than twenty minutes, Robyn had doled out the dog food and meat, while Rick filled the water dishes. Robyn took a few seconds to pat and speak to each dog. She never liked being away from them all day. Tomorrow Darby would probably spend most of the day here. Training runs and puppy lessons would fill the hours.

Rick walked with her back to the house. For a few seconds, everything felt in sync. If she could just forget about their finances, Grandpa's accident, and the buyer coming to look over her best dogs, life would be close to perfect right now.

❧

Robyn went about her chores in the dark Monday morning, trying not to think too hard about the day's schedule. The buyer was to arrive at nine a.m.

When she went inside after her morning feeding and cleanup, Mom was vacuuming the living room. She shut the vacuum off when Robyn came in. "Just slicking up a little. I'm glad we got the Christmas tree out of the house, but it left needles all over the rug."

Robyn didn't feel like doing anything special to get ready for the buyer, but that attitude would only show her immaturity. She raised her chin. "Do you want me to do anything to help?"

"No, just eat breakfast and try not to fret. Mr. Sterns will be here in an hour or so, and then we'll know one way or another if he wants to buy some dogs. Worrying about it won't change things."

"Mom—"

"Don't tell me you don't want to sell any dogs." Her mother put her hand to her temple and sighed. "I'm sorry, Robyn. The last few days have been. . ."

"I know. And I'm sorry." Robyn sat down on the arm of the couch. "I know it's been hard, going back and forth to see Grandpa. And I didn't like what the therapist said yesterday any better than you did."

Her mother came over and sat down in the chair opposite her. "Honey, we can't afford the skilled care for long. What little we had put away will be gone soon, but the physical therapist thinks Grandpa may need extended treatment."

Robyn nodded, mulling over what they'd heard the day before. "Six weeks, he said. Grandpa sure didn't like that."

"Neither do I," her mother admitted. "It's far longer than Dr. Mellin thought he'd need. But the therapist was right that Grandpa's still very weak. If he came home and took a bad fall, we'd be in a worse situation."

"So what can we do?"

"I hope they'll let us bring him home after a couple of weeks and drive him in for his appointments. Even using all that gas would be cheaper than keeping him in rehab."

"Mom, if we sell the breeding stock, our business will collapse." Robyn held her gaze and plunged on. "Selling good quality pups and trained sled dogs is our bread and butter. The race helps, but I don't see how we could continue running the Fire & Ice without a breeding kennel to support it. And your job isn't enough."

"I know all that." Mom pulled in a deep breath. "Sometimes I wonder if. . ."

"If what?"

"If we should sell the property and the business."

Robyn stared at her. "Everything? Sell the house and. . .no. We can't. What would we do? Where would we live?"

"I don't know, sweetie. I just think some days that we can't keep on the way we are."

"But. . .you don't want to move into Anchorage, do you? Get jobs there? Housing is really expensive in the city."

"That's true. And we own this place outright." Her mother ran a hand through her short, curly hair. "I don't know what to think. I just know things can't stay the same. I suppose we're better off in a house we own than paying rent. But with Grandpa's care. . ."

"Let's see what that social worker can tell us," Robyn said. "Dr. Mellin thought we might not be figuring right on the coverage. She said the government would use the patient's savings if insurance or Medicare won't pay for the treatment, but they can't take everything we have, too."

"You're right." Her mother stood and gave her a wan smile. "Hey, I'm going to do a little dusting in here. Why don't you eat something? And take off your jacket."

Robyn looked down at the grubby jacket she wore when she cleaned the dog pens. Usually when customers came, she changed her clothes and tried to look somewhat professional. Today she was so downhearted, she didn't really care if Mr. Sterns thought she looked scruffy.

As she poured milk on her cereal a few minutes later, she heard her mother's phone ring. If that was Philip Sterns, she was glad he had Mom's number, not hers. She didn't want to talk to him until she had to.

A lilt in her mother's tone drew her to the door between

the rooms. Mom smiled at her and mouthed, "Aven."

Her brother's name was the first thing to make her smile since Rick Baker's visit on Friday evening. Robyn did miss the traditional telephone, with extensions that allowed them all to share a conversation at once. She thought of asking Mom to use the speaker phone feature but instead concentrated on finishing her cereal. She'd get the details later.

Mom talked for a few minutes, giving Aven an update on Grandpa's condition. "That sounds great. Here, let me give the phone to Robyn. You can tell her yourself."

Robyn took it and put it to her ear. "Hey, how you doing?"

"Terrific. Caddie and I are planning to come up the Saturday before the race and stay all week. We want to spend some time with Grandpa and the rest of you."

"That's wonderful." Unexpected tears filled her eyes. "This is a good time for you to come."

"Oh? Better than usual?"

"We just need a little head-patting." Robyn wiped a tear away with her sleeve.

"Hey, kiddo, it's going to be okay. We'll talk everything over when I'm there."

She sniffed. "Good. Because Mom and I are kind of discouraged right now."

"I know. We're praying for you. We'll see you soon."

She signed off and handed the phone back to her mother. As she wiped away another tear, she smiled sheepishly. "Don't know why he makes me cry. I'm glad he's coming."

"Yes. Maybe he can help us make some decisions about your grandfather's care." Mom slid the phone into her pocket and held her arms out to Robyn. "Honey, I'm sorry that you're feeling so sad."

Robyn hugged her. "I don't mean to get upset. I just don't think this is a good time to think about selling our land and our dogs when they support us, even if we don't have much."

Her mother patted her back. "I know. Let's talk about this

later. I think I hear someone driving in."

"Oh, great!" Robyn stepped back. "My face is all blotchy, isn't it?"

Mom chuckled. "Go clean up. I'll offer him coffee."

❧

Philip Sterns stood when Robyn entered the room. That was a good sign, in her book. He looked to be about forty, with long, sturdy limbs. His hair receded off his forehead, and he wore glasses. Robyn tried not to form an opinion at first glance, but she didn't like him. His ears stuck out noticeably beyond the bows of his glasses, and his teeth looked overly white, like snow no one's walked on.

"Robyn is our head trainer now," her mother said as Robyn shook Sterns's hand. "My father-in-law helps her, but she's the boss."

"I'd be happy to show you the dogs I'm ready to sell," Robyn said. She put on her best jacket and led Sterns out the back door and to the dog lot.

"You have a gorgeous location." He looked appreciatively toward the mountain peaks.

"Thanks." She opened the gate to the enclosure for the adult male dogs. From puppies to retirees, all the dogs began barking as soon as they entered the yard. "Hush now," Robyn called softly, and the din subsided to an occasional yip.

"How do you make them do that?" Sterns asked.

She laughed. "One of the first things I teach my dogs is to be quiet unless there's something to bark about. Otherwise, our neighbors wouldn't be too happy."

"That's a pretty good trick."

"I understand you're new to dog sled racing," she said.

"Yes. A friend of mine took me to a couple of races in the Sierras last winter, and I fell in love with the sport. I've bought a couple of dogs, but I understand Alaskan huskies are the best."

"We like to think so, too."

He laughed. "I've done some research, and I'm thinking about doing some experimental breeding."

Robyn stopped with her hand on the latch of the gate. "How do you mean?"

"I'd like to try crossing huskies with some greyhound blood."

She nodded slowly. "Have you done any reading about that sort of crossbreeding?"

"A little. Oh, I know it's been tried before, but I have some ideas of my own."

"I see. Have you bred dogs before, Mr. Sterns? Or is this a new interest, since you became enamored of mushing?"

"I haven't actually raised any animals myself yet, but I want to. I've read that it's best to raise and train your own team. They know what you expect better that way."

"That can be true, but for someone new to the sport, it might be best to start with a team that's already mature and trained to mush. Get used to running the team, and make sure you like it. Then, if you want to get into breeding. . ."

"Oh, I know I like it." He grinned at her. "My friend let me drive his dogs a few times, and I'm hooked. What I'd really like to find is a team that's ready to go now, and I could do a few short races this spring. Then I can breed the dogs and start building my custom team. And next year. . .well, I'm thinking maybe I'll try to qualify for the big one."

"The. . .the Iditarod?"

"That's right. Oh, I know it takes years to master it, but I plan to be up there soon with Mackey and King and the rest."

Robyn swallowed hard. "That's quite a goal to work toward." She wanted to say more but decided to leave it alone. If he pursued the matter, he'd soon learn how tough it was to qualify for the Iditarod.

"This fellow is one of my best right now," she said, stooping to pat Max. She'd really miss him if she sold him, but the price she had in mind would pay for a lot of dog food. "He's a good lead dog, and he's strong."

"Is he. . .uh. . .can I breed him?"

"No, but—"

"I want to breed dogs and raise my own team," Sterns said, his face eager. "I'm serious about that."

"Mr. Sterns, I'm not really selling breeding stock right now. I raise dogs and train them to race. If I think they won't make good sled dogs, I sell them as pets. But I don't usually sell my breeding dogs."

"When I told your mother on the phone, she said you might need to sell a few."

Robyn's chest squeezed. "I'm sorry if there was a misunderstanding. That's not really my intent right now."

"Oh. Well. . .which one is your best sire? I did a little reading up on your kennel before I came. Isn't Tumble the one? Everyone wants pups with his bloodline, right?"

She hesitated then led him to Tumble's kennel. He greeted her with a quiet yip and licked her hand. "This is Tumble, and you're right. He's our primary sire right now. But he's not for sale."

She showed Sterns several other male dogs that did well in harness, but Rounder and the others didn't seem to impress him. Hero, a big black-and-white Siberian husky, bared his teeth and growled when the man approached him. The other dogs eyed Sterns with indifference. She took him over to the female dogs' enclosure. Coco ran to the end of her tether and strained eagerly toward them.

"Oh, I like this guy," Sterns said.

"She's four years old." Robyn determined to ignore his mistake. "She's a good team dog. I use her as a wheeler or anywhere else on the line except the lead. She's strong, and she has a lot of stamina. With a little more experience, she might work into lead, but right now I use her farther back."

"Has she had any litters?"

"Yes. One. I've got some of her pups I'm working with now." She thought about offering to sell him some of the female pups, but the idea of putting them into the hands of an inexperienced person for their sled training made her cringe.

After looking at half a dozen more females, Sterns nodded and shoved his hands in his pockets. "I like them all. What do you say I take those three"—he nodded toward Coco and the two others nearest her—"and Tumble."

Robyn sucked in a deep breath. "Tumble isn't for sale. I can give you one of his sons—a two-year-old showing a lot of promise." She supposed she could sell three adult females and be all right. But Tumble was out of the question.

"I'll tell you what." He smiled and peered at her through his glasses. "I'll meet your price on all the females without any dickering. And for Tumble, I'll give you triple what you're asking for the two-year-old."

Robyn's heart sank. How could she turn down that kind of money when they needed it so badly? If Mom were out here with them, she'd probably accept the offer. But it would set Robyn's breeding program back years. Tumble's offspring were becoming known in racing circles. Mushers noticed his pups wherever they ran, which would include the Yukon Quest and the Iditarod this year. She wanted to be ready when they won. She had no doubt more dog owners would bring their females to Holland Kennels for breeding.

She swallowed hard. "I'm sorry, Mr. Sterns. I stand by what I said. You can bring your females here to be bred, but Tumble isn't for sale."

He studied her for a long moment. "How about if I go back to Anchorage and give you a couple of days to think it over? Talk to your mother about it. I'll come back Wednesday."

"I won't change my mind."

"Are you sure about that?" He smiled again. "I'm not prepared to take the dogs I buy today, anyway. I've got a rental car. I'll have to come back with a truck."

"We can crate and ship the dogs for you, if you want. We've trucked dogs to the airport for our customers before. It's no problem. But I really think Max is a better dog for you. You said you'd like a lead dog you can race this spring."

He shook his head. "I still think we should let this sit for a couple of days. We'll talk again Wednesday."

four

After supper Robyn hitched up six dogs for a two-mile run. The snow was eighteen inches deep on open areas, and the trail conditions were perfect. Mom had gone to Anchorage and would be back later, after Robyn got home.

Half a mile out, just after she crossed onto Rick's land, Tumble barked and surged forward. The other dogs caught his energy and pulled faster, too. Soon Robyn saw what inspired them. Someone with a flashlight was coming toward them on snowshoes.

She recognized Rick as they reached him. He stepped off the trail and waited for her to stop the team. Robyn set the snow hook and greeted him.

Rick pushed back his hood and grinned at her. "You're looking good. How's it going?"

"Well, Mom called a little while ago and said Grandpa did well on his therapy sessions today. But they're still giving him pain meds for aches and pains."

"It takes the old bones longer to heal than it does young ones."

"Yeah."

"Did the buyer come to look over your dogs?"

She nodded. "Philip Sterns. I don't like him. He doesn't know much about dogs, but he wants to race this year and he thinks that by next year he'll qualify for the Iditarod."

"Hmm. Does he have someone to mentor him?"

"I'm not sure. He did mention some friends who got him interested in sledding, but he's not ready to own good dogs, Rick. He'll ruin them."

"So you don't want to sell to him."

"Not really, but. . .the truth is, we need the cash, and Mom is pushing me to close the deal. He's coming back Wednesday."

"How many dogs does he want?"

"Four in all. I don't have much problem with selling him three females, although he'll probably mess up their training. But he wants to start his own designer breeding program, and he knows absolutely nothing about dogs."

"That's tough to accept."

"I'll say. And he wants to buy Tumble. I told him and Mom absolutely not, but. . .well, he's offering us a bundle for him." The team was restless and wriggled in their harnesses. "I shouldn't stop long. They want to run, and they deserve it. But thanks for letting me sound off."

"Sounds like you have a tough decision to make," Rick said. "I'll keep praying for you."

"Thanks. I admit I get riled when I think about selling off our breeding stock. The business would go under."

"And your mom wants to do that? Does she want to get out of the kennel business?"

Robyn sighed. "I don't know. But she pointed out today that we may end up having to sell everything anyway, and it would be better to sell the best dogs now at a good price than to wait and have to sell in a hurry at reduced figures when we're desperate."

"I'm sorry. I had no idea things were that bad."

"I'm not sure they are, but Mom seems to think that Grandpa's situation will break us. I don't know much about insurance and Medicare and all that, but it doesn't seem fair. Sometimes I wonder if she's just tired of this life and wants to move into town."

Rick's eyes widened. "You mean. . .sell your house and everything?"

"She's mentioned it. Please keep that between us. I don't think it's going to happen, but when Mom gets fretting about money, she says things like that."

"That's a lot to deal with." He cocked his head to one side. "Do you think maybe you don't like this Sterns fellow because making a deal with him could signal the end of your family's way of life, or do you have something specific not to like about him?"

"Besides the fact that he's green as grass?" She thought about it for a moment. "He came with a pocketful of cash, but that's not really unusual. People know they can't always use a credit card or write a check out here in the hinterlands. I guess the thing I like least is the way the dogs reacted to him. They didn't seem to take to him." She looked up and smiled ruefully. "That and the fact that he has fancy clothes and is staying at the swankiest hotel in Anchorage."

"Mmm. Real 'dog racing' people don't usually put on airs."

"Yeah. Is he a rich guy who fancies getting into a hobby that will make him look rugged to his friends?"

"People like that usually tire of it when they learn how much work is involved."

"Exactly," she said. "Then what will become of these beautiful dogs?"

❧

Rick stepped closer to Robyn—as close as his unwieldy snowshoes would let him. He laid his gloved hand on the sleeve of her parka.

"Listen, I don't know if this would help you or not, but I'll be in Anchorage all day tomorrow. I have a friend with the state police, and I was thinking. . ."

Her eyes glistened with what might be hope, so he plunged on.

"He may not be able to do anything, but I could ask him to look into this guy's background and just make sure he's legit."

"Wow, that would make me feel better. Even if they didn't find anything—I mean, if he doesn't have a police record, that's good, right?"

She gave him Sterns's full name, the hotel where he was lodging, his cell phone number, and the town in California where he claimed he lived. Rick was glad to be able to do something to help her. His concern for the Hollands had grown over the last few days, and he wanted to take away some of Robyn's anxiety.

The dogs whined, and she reached for the snow hook. "We need to get going. Thanks for listening, Rick."

"Anytime. And be careful. I saw a moose not far from here yesterday."

"Okay, I'll stay alert. Don't want a moose tearing into my team."

He watched her and the sled team move down the trail into the trees. *She'll be okay*, he told himself. Though he'd heard of a few instances where a moose had savaged a dog team that couldn't escape its wrath, that was a rare happening. Usually the huge animals lumbered into the woods as soon as they saw someone coming. And Robyn knew what she was doing. He was more worried about her financial straits.

He was beginning to care for her beyond friendship, and he didn't like to think that her family might leave the area. His friend Joel Dawes might not be able to help him out. Maybe he should have broached the subject to Joel before mentioning it to Robyn, but her uneasiness about the potential sale to Sterns had overcome his caution. Assurance that the prospective buyer was honest should help Robyn feel easier about selling some of her treasured dogs to him.

Rick set out once more on his snowshoes, mulling over the Hollands' situation. If Cheryl seriously wanted to sell the property, he wouldn't mind adding to his own land. But he didn't suppose he had enough money for that. Opening his new practice in Wasilla last year had tied up all his savings. He wondered, too, who owned the Hollands' property. Robyn's father had died in an accident several years earlier. A plane crash, if he remembered correctly. Was the deed in

Cheryl's name—or Grandpa Steve's?

An hour later he got home and built up his wood fire. Relaxing with a cup of cocoa and a handful of cookies from a store package, he found that he couldn't stop thinking of Robyn. When he considered his hours spent at Far North Veterinary, it now bore directly on the amount of time he had available to spend with her. The drive to the city on Sunday for church tired him out and took him away from his Wasilla patients—and Robyn. Definitely time to focus his efforts.

He looked at his watch. She'd have put the dogs away by now and buttoned down the kennel for the night. He pulled out his phone. "Hey, Robyn? It's Rick." He felt suddenly like he was back in high school, calling a girl from chem lab and wondering what to say next. "Just wanted to see how your ride went."

"Good. No moose that I saw. And I'm pleased with the way the dogs are progressing."

"Glad to hear it." He loved the way she talked about her dogs—businesslike, but with the pride of a mother.

"I'm thinking of entering a short race next month, after we're done with the craziness here," she said. "It's a great way to get the dogs used to competition and crowds."

"Sounds like fun."

"Hey, do you remember what I told you earlier, about. . . about our property?"

"Yes." He sensed that she didn't want to say too much over the phone.

"Well, my mom says Sterns is interested."

"In the whole place?"

"Yes. I'm having a hard time with this. It makes me furious that she told someone like him—someone we know nothing about."

"Did she talk to him again since this morning?"

"Apparently he called her tonight, after she left the nursing home. She phoned me on her way home. She hasn't gotten here yet, but. . .well, you promised to pray for me. Would you pray that I don't have a rip-roaring, knock-down-drag-out with my mom?"

"Yes. I surely will. I'll do that right now. And I won't forget tomorrow. If I can find out anything about this guy for you, I'll call you."

He hung up still feeling her alarm. Would trying to help her put him in the middle of a bitter family dispute?

ॐ

Robyn waited up for her mother, her anger simmering. She planned what she would say when Mom walked through the door. This wasn't fair. Robyn's name might not be on the deed to the property, but she ought to have a say in what became of her home and her business.

Even though her thoughts made sense to her, she knew her attitude was wrong. Mom had worked hard, even before Dad died. She'd helped in the kennel business, too, but had finally taken the job at the store to supplement their erratic income. When it came right down to it, Mom had probably suffered most of all the family.

She'd moved with her husband and two-year-old son from civilized Pennsylvania to the wilds of Alaska. She never complained about the cold or the light deprivation and the seasonal affective disorder some Alaska residents—especially the transplants—suffered. She pitched in and helped.

Grandpa's accident was a case in point. Mom was dealing with it the best way she knew how. Getting Grandpa the best treatment they could. Visiting him as often as possible, though the forty-five-mile drive from their home in Wasilla to the nursing home in Anchorage took an hour each way.

Robyn tried to focus on her anger once more. She stopped before the front door and practiced the words she had planned to say. "What were you thinking, Mom? Telling a stranger we're considering selling our home when Grandpa doesn't even know yet."

Oh yes, those words would cut deep. In her own ears, she sounded rude, disrespectful, and childish.

Tears flooded her eyes, and she flopped down on the sofa.

When her mother came in twenty minutes later, Robyn met her with a tender heart. She threw her arms around her. "Mom, I'm sorry I was mad at you. Can we talk about this?"

"Of course." Her mom took her coat and gloves off and sat down beside her. "I know it's hard for you to think about moving away from here. This has been your only home."

"Yes. But I—"

Mom held up one hand. "Haven't you ever wondered what it would be like to live someplace else? Someplace. . .easier?"

Robyn stared at her. "You mean, outside Alaska?"

"Yes."

"No." Robyn let out a puff of breath and looked away. The conversation had nose-dived so fast she felt dizzy.

"I thought a lot about it on the way home," Mom said. "I realize I shouldn't have mentioned to Mr. Sterns that we might sell our property before the family had discussed it thoroughly. He caught me by surprise when he said he was looking at land and thinking of moving up here, and I just. . . let it fall out of my mouth. That was wrong of me."

Robyn shook her head. "I thought maybe you were just tired of the dogs and never having any money."

Her mother laughed with a sniff. "Honey, I love dogs. It's true, sometimes I wonder how we'll get by, and I do get sick of vacuuming up dog hair, but our life here has been pretty good these last twenty-five years, don't you think? What you can remember of them, that is."

"Well, yeah." Robyn reflected that she had never known anything else. What if she'd grown up in Pennsylvania, or some other place that had even less snow? She would still love animals, of that she was sure. But what if she'd never had the opportunity to go dog sledding? "If you and Grandpa really think we should move, then I guess we should. But I can't imagine being happier somewhere else. And Grandpa. . . do you think he would even consider moving south?"

"You're probably right. He'd hate it." Mom sat for a moment, staring down at the rug. Then she smiled. "I don't know how God is going to work this out, but I believe He will."

"So. . ." Robyn eyed her cautiously. "You're willing to tell Mr. Sterns that we don't want to sell this place?"

"Yes. Unless Grandpa wants to sell it. It's half his, after all."

Robyn nodded. "Thank you."

Her mother held out her arms, and Robyn hugged her.

"Mom, I know keeping the kennel going has been hard on you. You've worked constantly since Dad died, and I appreciate that."

Her mother turned and grabbed a tissue from a box on the end table. "There have been some difficult moments. I won't deny that. The financial worries have been stressful. But, you know what? Even when I'm worrying, I know that's wrong. God doesn't want me to wear myself out worrying. What do you say we pray about this together?"

"Yes. And maybe tomorrow I can go with you to Anchorage, and we can talk to Grandpa and see what he thinks."

"That's a good idea. In fact, why don't I call the store tonight and see if it's possible for me to work an earlier shift tomorrow? If I could get out, say, by three, we could drive into town and see Grandpa and eat supper in Anchorage."

"Can we afford it?"

"Well, I was thinking fast food, not a fancy restaurant."

Robyn nodded. "Yeah. Let's do it. I'll get Darby to feed the dogs their supper."

"Can she handle it alone?"

"I think so. I'll have the meat ready and leave her lots of notes."

Her mother laughed and seized her hand. "Let's pray now."

five

Rick made a house call at a dairy farm on his way to the clinic Tuesday morning. He also stopped to see a client's injured Irish setter. Heading once more for the animal hospital, he realized he would drive past the hotel where Philip Sterns was staying. On a whim, he drove into the parking area and strolled to the lobby.

At the desk, he told the clerk he was looking for Sterns.

"I'm sorry, I can't give you his room number," the young woman replied, "but if you'd like, I can call his room and see if he's in."

Rick hesitated. What would he say?

"Oh, there he is now." The clerk nodded toward the elevators.

Rick swung around and saw a thin, middle-aged man step out and head toward the main entrance.

"Thanks." He hurried to catch up with him. "Mr. Sterns?"

"Yes?" The man stopped walking and turned toward him.

"Hi. I'm Rick Baker." He extended his hand, and the man shook it. "Uh, I understand you're looking for property in the area."

"Are you a real estate agent?"

"No." Rick smiled sheepishly. "Actually, I'm a veterinarian. But I do know someone who's in the real estate business—the agent who helped me find my place in Wasilla last year."

Sterns eyed him curiously through his glasses. "And how did you get my name?"

"I'm sorry. I probably should have started with that. I'm a neighbor of the Hollands."

"Ah." He relaxed visibly and Rick felt more confident.

"Cheryl and Robyn are friends of mine, and they mentioned they'd had a visitor who was looking for property. Since I work close by, I thought I'd drop in and see if you'd found an agent to work with."

"Yes, as a matter of fact, I'm on my way out to meet with one now."

"Oh, well, you're all set then." Rick felt a little silly, but he was glad he'd gotten a look at the man. He was sharper than Rick had suspected, given Robyn's description.

"Wasilla is one of the areas I'm considering when I relocate," Sterns said. "Perhaps you could give me the agent's name. If I don't find what I want down here, I may do some serious looking up there."

"Sure." Rick wrote down the name of the agency for him.

"Do you treat the Hollands' dogs?"

Rick nodded. "When they need it. They're a healthy lot."

"So, as far as you know, their dogs wouldn't have any problems? I'm looking at some of their adult females and one male, Tumble."

"Oh, yes, I know Tumble. He's in great shape. I don't know a kennel with a better health record." Rick eyed the man once more but could think of no way to get useful information from him without arousing suspicion.

"The girl, Robyn," Sterns said, frowning. "She seems reluctant to sell them."

"Robyn loves her dogs, but she's a businesswoman. If she thinks it's best for her kennel, she'll sell you the dogs you want. If not, then she'll offer you others of comparable quality." Rick stepped back. "I'd better head on over to the animal hospital. Nice to meet you."

Sterns nodded and walked out the door. Rick inhaled deeply. He should have asked Joel's assistance first, and not tried to meet Sterns. If the man was underhanded, he'd be suspicious now. And Rick had admitted that the Hollands had talked about him. That might not sit so well. He wished he'd thought of a way to get out of revealing that.

He pulled out his cell phone as he walked to his pickup. Sterns passed him in a red rental car. Rick waved, but Sterns ignored him.

"Hey, Joel? This is Rick Baker. Are you able to access databases to find out some background information on someone from another state?"

಼

Robyn drove toward Anchorage with her mother beside her.

Mom was content to let her drive and was even happier when Aven phoned. After chatting for about ten minutes with him, she put the headset on her phone and passed it to Robyn.

"Hey," Robyn said. "What's up?"

"You're not driving in heavy traffic while you talk, are you?" her big brother asked.

"No, I'm on the Glenn Highway, and traffic's light."

"Okay. I guess you heard Mom telling me about this guy who's interested in the land."

"Yeah, I did. What do you think about that?"

"I told Mom to do whatever she thinks she has to do."

"I agree, mostly. If we really need to sell, then she and Grandpa should do it. Mom and I talked a lot last night. I think the question is, do we need to be thinking about this now?"

"Well, Caddie and I are agreed that we should try to help you if we can."

"No, that's not right. You shouldn't be helping support us." Robyn looked at her mother, and Mom shook her head adamantly. "Listen, you've sent us part of your pay ever since you joined the Coast Guard. But you have your own family to think of now. It's time for us to stand on our own feet and for you and Caddie to invest your income in your own family."

"Well. . .we'll talk about it when we come for the race. But keep me posted on this guy, okay? Because if you don't want to sell the land, you need to be firm, and if that upsets him and kills the sale of the dogs. . ."

"We can handle it," Robyn said, but she wasn't sure how. She passed the phone and headset back to her mother.

"You know what, honey?" her mom said to Aven. "We're going to talk this over with Grandpa tonight. After we've discussed all the options, we'll be able to make a better decision about it."

Robyn sighed and tried to concentrate on the road.

"You know," Mom said after she had hung up, "when Rick called this morning and you were in the shower—"

"What about it?" Robyn asked. She'd scurried as quickly as she could to take the brief call. Rick had inquired about her grandfather and their plans and then signed off to drive to work.

"We chatted for a couple of minutes, and he mentioned that he's still going to church in Anchorage, but he wants to stop driving that far, even though he'll miss his friends there."

"Really?" Robyn stared at her. Had Mom been doing a little snooping on her behalf?

"I invited him to visit our church any time. It wouldn't surprise me if he showed up some Sunday."

Robyn said nothing but wondered how she would handle things if Rick walked into their church on Sunday. She was glad for the warning.

Twenty minutes later they reached the nursing home. Grandpa was eating an early supper from a tray.

"They say they'll have me up and eating in the dining room within a few days," he said after greeting them. "I'm not sure I want to."

"What's wrong?" Mom asked.

"I think they need a new cook. Cheryl, I miss your cooking. Did you bring me anything?"

Mom laughed and opened her tote bag. "Robyn made some brownies this morning while I was at work, though when she had time, I don't know. She's busy all the time without you there to help her."

"That's right." Robyn passed the plastic container of brownies to him. "We're in high gear, getting ready for the race. I need you, so hurry up and get better."

He fumbled with the container, and Robyn leaned over to help him open it.

"So what's going on at home?" Grandpa asked. "Didn't you have a buyer coming yesterday?"

"Yes, he came," Cheryl said.

"How many dogs is he taking?"

Robyn smiled at his assumption. "He wants four, but I don't want to sell one of them."

"Which one?"

"He's got his eye on Tumble."

"What? You can't sell Tumble." Grandpa pushed up on his elbow and scowled at her. "Did you tell him you'd sell our top stud dog?"

"No, Grandpa. I didn't. But of course he saw Tumble when we went into the yard, and he took to him. He said he'd read about us before he came, and he might have had the idea in his mind all along to make an offer for Tumble."

"Well, he can't have him."

Robyn looked at her mother.

"Fine. We'll tell him that Tumble is absolutely not for sale. But, Dad. . ."

"What?" Grandpa lay back on the pillow, not entirely mollified. "That's what comes of having that Web site. Everybody and his brother can look on there and see our best dogs."

"That's advertising," Robyn reminded him.

"Yes," her mother added. "A lot of people look at that site. The pictures of the dogs are the next best thing to seeing the actual dogs. I think it's brought in quite a bit of business."

"You think we should sell Tumble?"

"Not necessarily, but. . ." Mom cleared her throat. "You

know things have been tight lately. I may be able to get a few more hours per week at the store, but. . ."

"No," he said. "We don't want you working more. I hate that you have to work away from home. If Dan was still alive, he wouldn't hear of it."

Mom pressed her lips together and looked toward the window.

"What?" Grandpa said again. "Is it worse than I know about?" When Cheryl still didn't meet his gaze, he turned to stare at Robyn.

Her breath caught, and she started to speak but stopped. Were their financial straits as bad as Mom thought they were? She wished she could say with certainty that everything would be all right, but she didn't dare.

After a long moment, Grandpa sighed. "I see. It's me. My medical expenses. Well, I tell you what, I can walk out of here today. I don't have to stay in here six weeks, or even two weeks, no matter what that therapist says." He threw back the bedclothes and thrust his legs over the side of the bed.

"No, Grandpa," Robyn said quickly. She reached to take his arm, but he had already pushed off the bed.

Almost at once his knees buckled, and he collapsed against her.

Mom stifled a cry and leaped to help Robyn get him back on the bed.

He lay there with his eyes nearly closed, panting.

"Let's not have any more stunts like that one," Mom said in a tight voice. "You need this treatment. I won't argue about it."

"You can't sell off all the dogs," he choked. "Robyn knows which ones she needs to keep and which ones to let go. Don't you, Robby?"

"Yes, Grandpa." She took his hand and squeezed it.

"Dad. . ." Mom's face radiated pain as she looked down at him. Her eyes glistened, and tears spilled down her cheeks.

"Don't cry," he said. "We'll sell a few dogs and we'll get by."

Slowly Mom sat down. "I guess this would not be a good time to suggest selling the homestead."

Grandpa stared at her for a long moment, then looked away. No one spoke for a minute.

"Grandpa, I don't think we need to think about that," Robyn said softly. "If the bills are too big, then I could get a job, too. And if we need to sell more dogs, we will, though I'd like to keep our foundation stock so that we can keep breeding. But if worse comes to worst—"

"She's right," Mom said. "I never should have considered it. I'll tell Mr. Sterns—"

"Who?"

"The man who's buying the dogs. I'll tell him we're not selling the house."

"Wait, wait, wait." Grandpa grabbed her sleeve. "The man buying the dogs—the one who wants Tumble—also wants to buy our property?"

Mom shifted uneasily. "He mentioned that he was looking for a place in the area. But I can see you don't want to consider that."

"What would we do?" Grandpa asked. "Where would we live?"

"I. . .don't know."

Robyn's throat constricted as she watched Grandpa's face. The unspoken thought hung in the air—that he might never go home to live with them again.

"I'd like to meet this fellow," he said.

"Oh, that's not necessary." Mom leaned forward, her brow furrowed. "I'll explain to him that I spoke prematurely. And I'm sorry. Truly sorry. I hadn't stopped to consider how you or Robyn would feel before I mentioned it to him."

"No, I'm serious." Grandpa nodded. "If things are bad enough to make you think like that, then maybe we do need to take drastic measures. And even if we're not selling more than a few team dogs to this man, I'd like to get a look at him. I'm a pretty good judge of character. I'd like to talk to him and make sure he knows how to handle good dogs. I won't sell—or let Robyn sell—Holland dogs to just anyone. I'd rather starve first."

Robyn's pride welled up, and she wiped an errant tear from her cheek. She'd seen Grandpa turn away a buyer once because he'd heard the man treated his dogs poorly. "I love you, Grandpa." She leaned down and kissed the top of his head.

Mom let out a sigh and managed a wobbly smile. "All right. Shall I call him and see if he can come here to meet you? He's staying nearby in a hotel."

"Sure," Grandpa said. "I'll put on my best bathrobe."

Robyn laughed. "I'll help you get ready. Anything you need, just ask me." She looked at her mother. "And thanks, Mom. I think we'll all feel better if Grandpa's in on this decision."

"You could handle the sale by yourself," Grandpa said grudgingly. "You know enough about dogs—what they're capable of and exactly what they're worth."

"Thanks for trusting me, but as you said, you're a pretty good judge of people."

"That's because I've been around so long and met so many of them."

Mom excused herself and went out into the hallway to call Mr. Sterns.

A staff member came in and retrieved Grandpa's supper tray.

"You okay?" Grandpa asked Robyn.

"Yeah. I was pretty keyed up about this, but Mom and I prayed about it last night. We agreed we needed to bring you in on it. I'm glad you're going to meet Mr. Sterns."

"What's he like?"

She shrugged. "I don't like him, but I'm trying not to pass judgment on him unfairly. He doesn't know a lot about dogs, and he's just getting into sledding. He wants to do some racing right away. I've got to wonder if he wouldn't work the dogs too hard at first."

"Hmm. That can happen." Grandpa opened the brownie box and held it out toward her. "Have one?"

"No, those are for you. We've got more at home." He took one and she replaced the cover on the box.

Mom came back, wearing a businesslike smile. "Mr. Sterns would be happy to meet you. He's having dinner with his real estate agent, but he can come by here around seven."

Grandpa looked at the clock on the wall opposite the bed. "Why don't you two go and eat? You've got almost two hours. You can get back in plenty of time."

Mom looked at Robyn, and she nodded.

"All right, but you have to promise not to try to get up alone."

He frowned at his daughter-in-law. "Me? Would I do that?"

Mom swatted lightly at his shoulder.

"We'd better go." Robyn jumped up. "See you later, alligator—and we're serious. Be good."

They drove around the corner for hamburgers and milkshakes. Robyn wondered if Mom was reluctant to spend even a few dollars for the meal. She tried to keep the conversation on pleasant topics and described how well Darby was doing in her sled driving lessons.

Mom waited in the nursing home lobby for Sterns while Robyn went to Grandpa's room to make sure he was ready. She helped him get his robe on. He wanted to move to the armchair, so Robyn called one of the staffers to help her, and they got him situated. She had to admit, he looked stronger and more capable sitting in the chair than he had lying down.

As the staffer straightened the bedclothes, Mom led Philip Sterns in and introduced him to Grandpa, a strained smile on her face.

"So, you want to buy some Holland Kennel dogs," Grandpa said affably.

"Yes, sir. I made a list of three good breeding kennels before I flew up here, and yours was the top one. I knew the minute your granddaughter showed me your dog yard that I'd come to the right place."

"That right?"

"Oh, yes. Everything's shipshape. And your dogs have wonderful bloodlines. I read up on your dogs' performances. That Chick line is what I want."

Grandpa smiled. "Then I guess you know our Tumble is one of Chick's sons."

"He's a fine-looking dog, and I think he's perfect for my foundation stock."

"So you want to breed dogs, as well as race." Grandpa shook his head, still smiling. "That's ambitious."

"I know. But I never do things by halves."

"Well, sir, why don't you sit right down here and tell me about your experience with sled dogs. What sort of setup do you have in California?"

Grandpa knew the right questions to ask. Sterns soon relaxed and talked freely. After twenty minutes of talk about dogs, Grandpa brought up the property matter.

"Sounds like you might do all right if you start with well-trained dogs and have someone to advise you when you need it. But just so you know, I'm not ready to sell my property. My son and I bought the place twenty-five years ago, and it's home. Cheryl and I talked about it a little tonight, and I just don't want to sell."

"That's perfectly all right," Sterns assured him. "I've been out all day looking at land, and I've seen a couple of places that might do for me."

Grandpa nodded. "Well, Cheryl can hang on to your contact information in case we decide to sell later on, but for the time being, the Hollands are staying put."

The nurse entered the room with a clipboard in her hand. "I'm sorry, folks, but Mr. Holland needs some rest now."

"I'm sure he does." Robyn jumped up, ready to help get Grandpa back to bed if she was needed.

Sterns said to Cheryl, "I'll come up to Wasilla in the morning, then, and get the four dogs I'm buying, if that's all right with you."

"Uh, Mr. Sterns?" Robyn shot a quick glance at Grandpa.

"Yes?"

"We're keeping Tumble. Grandpa and I agree he's an essential part of Holland Kennel right now."

Grandpa nodded. "That's right. Tumble has never been for sale. But we can offer you one of his sons who would—"

A flicker of darkness crossed Sterns's face and he exhaled sharply. "I thought we had a deal."

Mom stepped forward with a look of alarm. "I believe you asked Robyn to think it over."

"You've wasted my time."

Robyn said hastily, "I'm sorry, sir, but we're keeping Tumble. We haven't advertised him for sale, and I told you yesterday I didn't want to sell him. If that means you don't want the three female dogs, either. . ."

He looked at her sharply then flicked a glance toward Grandpa, who sagged a little in his chair.

"Folks," the nurse said, "I really must ask you to leave."

Sterns locked gazes with Robyn again. "I'll let you know tomorrow."

six

Sterns exited abruptly, and Robyn and her mother kissed Grandpa good night and left.

"Mom, I'm sorry things went badly in there," Robyn said as they walked toward the car.

"No, honey, don't be. You were wonderful. He was rude and made assumptions he shouldn't have made. I'll be glad to see the back of him tomorrow."

"Me, too."

Mom smiled at her as she unlocked the car. "Are you sure you want to sell him any of your babies?"

Robyn swallowed hard. "I think we have to. We need to order more meat for the dogs, and we'll have a lot of expenses while we get ready for the race. But I'm glad Grandpa wouldn't sell Tumble."

"So am I," Mom admitted. "He personally raised that dog, and I know Tumble is one of his favorites."

Robyn drove home and found Darby's note saying her father had driven her over and helped her feed all of the dogs their suppers. The temperature had dropped to ten below zero. Robyn made a brief round of the kennels and made sure all of the animals were snug in their shelters. She'd put extra straw bedding in the doghouses that morning, and all were settled down for the night. The puppies slept together in a jumbled pile in their communal shelter. She checked the padlock on the barn, reflecting that if Sterns didn't buy the dogs he'd picked out, she'd have to dip into her meager savings account to pay for the next shipment of dog food.

Snow began to fall as she went into the house. She took off her boots and work jacket near the back door.

Her mother, already in her bathrobe, sat at the kitchen table with a mug of tea. "Everything okay?"

"Yes," Robyn said. She walked to the stove and lifted the teakettle. It held plenty of hot water, so she opened the cupboard to get herself a mug. As she turned around, the glow of headlights swept over the walls.

"Someone's here." Her mother rose and walked to the window. "Looks like Rick's truck. I'm not dressed for company. Would you mind if I disappeared?"

"That's fine." A shiver of anticipation propelled Robyn to the front door before he even knocked. Over the last few days, Rick had paid a lot of attention to her and her family. Was it just neighborliness, or was her wish coming true? In the midst of the stress and sadness she'd encountered, Rick was the one bright spot of her days. But she didn't dare count on that continuing. If he backed off once this crisis passed, the disappointment would be too great.

&

Rick drove into the Hollands' yard at nine o'clock Tuesday night. Ordinarily he wouldn't call so late, but he knew Cheryl and Robyn had spent the afternoon and evening in Anchorage, and the lights were still on at their house.

As he climbed the steps to the front deck, Robyn opened the door. Her long, dark hair hung loose about her shoulders, and she wore black pants and a green sweater. Usually he saw her in jeans and a thick jacket, but this softer outfit gave her a decidedly feminine air.

His pulse quickened, and he smiled. "Hi. Is it too late? I just wanted to tell you what I learned today."

"No, come on in. We haven't been home long, and I was making myself some tea. Want some?"

"Sure." He followed her to the kitchen, unzipping his jacket.

She opened a cookie jar shaped like a husky and put a handful of cookies on a plate then fixed him a cup of tea to go with hers.

"How's Coco doing?" he asked.

"Good. She's one of the three Sterns wants to buy." Robyn made a face as though she'd tasted foul medicine. "Just thought I'd warn you, since you've gotten friendly with her."

Rick winced. "Did you plan to sell her?"

"I'm not against it. I'd rather sell some of the extra males that we've trained as team dogs, but he wants females, so. . . ."

"I came to talk to you about Sterns."

"Did your friend find out anything?"

He nodded, hating to bring bad news but knowing she'd feel somewhat vindicated for being uneasy about the man. "Joel discovered that Philip Sterns has been in prison in California for fraud and theft."

"You're joking." Robyn tossed her dark hair back and brought the sugar bowl over from the counter. "Do you want milk?"

"No, thanks. I told Joel I wanted to make sure the information he got was for the same man. He brought a picture of the guy over to the clinic for me to look at. It's him."

"How did you recognize him?" She sat down opposite him.

Rick hesitated. "I stopped at the hotel this morning, and I got a look at him. But Joel didn't find any outstanding warrants on him." He picked up his mug and sipped the hot, strong tea.

"What does that mean? He's not a fugitive?"

"As far as we know, he's done his time and he's free now."

She shook her head. "I don't know about you, but I feel as though we've had a narrow escape. Mom was actually thinking about selling the property to this guy."

"I. . .didn't know she owned it." Rick said quickly, "I don't mean to pry. I'd just assumed Steve. . ."

"Grandpa owns half." Robyn reached for a cookie. "Mom and Dad owned half together before Dad died. Grandpa had invested in the land with Dad when they first came here."

"I see." He could also tell that the situation was taking a

toll on her. Her eyelids drooped, and she seemed to consider her words carefully. He wished he could assure her that everything would be all right, but he couldn't do that.

"We told Grandpa all about Sterns," she said, "and he wanted to meet him, so Mom called him. He came over to the nursing home. Grandpa told him the property's not for sale, and he was okay with that. But when I said we aren't selling Tumble either, he got kind of nasty."

"I'm sorry to hear that."

"Yeah. We don't like the idea of selling any dogs to him, but he walked out saying he'd let us know tomorrow if he still wanted Coco and the others." Her dark eyes held misgivings as she took a bite of her cookie.

"You could still say no."

"If he wants to buy and I told him now that I don't want to sell. . ." She shook her head. "He was a little scary tonight."

Rick wished he could do something concrete to comfort her, but the situation seemed beyond his control. He did know Someone with greater power though. "I've been praying about your situation."

"That means a lot." She smiled at him, and his heart lurched.

"I'm glad Steve and Cheryl don't see a need to sell the property. I'm sure God will find a way for your family to get through this rough spot." He was glad he hadn't jumped in with an offer to buy them out. That probably would have upset Robyn and her grandfather even more. It was just as well that his assets were tied up. He took a cookie and bit into it.

"Grandpa's determined to stick it out here," Robyn said. "He was shocked when Mom hinted at leaving Alaska."

"Well, maybe you should just wait and see what happens. The Lord knows what's ahead. I'm sure He's got something planned for the Hollands."

She nodded slowly. "Sterns is supposed to come tomorrow if

he wants to buy. If not, he'll call. I'm not sure I'll wait around all day to see if he shows up. I've got a lot to do for the race."

"What's on your list for tomorrow?"

"Putting up markers on part of the race route. Of course, if we get a lot of snow out of this storm, I may have to wait."

"I don't think this will amount to much." Rick glanced toward the window. "It's too cold for a really big snow."

"Well then, I'll probably try to get the hilly part marked tomorrow."

The opportunity to be with her and perhaps help her in a small way beckoned him. He asked casually, "Want someone to tag along?"

She arched her eyebrows. "What, you want to ride on my sled?"

"I've mushed in my time. Had a team before I went away to vet school."

"So, you're saying you'd go along if I supply you a team?"

"I guess that's a little presumptuous."

"No, it's not. We have an extra sled. If you're serious, it might be fun."

Rick smiled at her. "I haven't driven a team for a while, but I used to know what I was doing. It would be an honor to mush with you."

"Great. Hey, wait a minute. Isn't tomorrow one of your days in Anchorage?"

"They need me Thursday this week, so I switched." He frowned as he remembered Bob's and Hap's reactions when he'd told them two days a week in Anchorage was too much for him. After next week he was going back to Tuesdays only. They hadn't liked it one bit. Rick had even told them that his goal, as much as he liked them, was to stop working at Far North altogether and put his energy into his own practice.

"So you're free all day?"

"I could go with you in the morning. I've got a few barn calls I need to make after lunch, but if you're sure you trust me to drive some of your dogs, I'd love to go out on the trail with you."

"Sure. Call me by eight. If the weather's not good, or if Sterns has scheduled a time to come, I'll tell you. Otherwise, we can go then."

"Sounds good." Rick finished his tea.

"Want some more?"

"No, I'd better head home and get some sleep. I have to hit the trail in the morning, and the boss musher is strict about punctuality."

She laughed, and Rick's anticipation level soared. If he could have imagined the perfect way to spend his free morning, sledding with Robyn would have been beyond the most appealing thing he'd have come up with.

He leaned across the table and squeezed her hand. "Thanks for trusting me. I may be too keyed up to sleep."

"You'd *better* sleep. I don't want you falling asleep on the runners tomorrow."

❧

The next morning, conditions were perfect for sledding. Robyn hurried to feed all the dogs and make sure the equipment was ready. As she worked, her thoughts bounced continually to Rick. His generous offers of help lately gave her spirits a boost, and the fact that he wanted to go sledding with her. . .just thinking about it made her breathe faster. He must like her as more than a client and neighbor. The way he'd looked at her last night had propelled her dreams into high gear.

At about seven thirty the back door to the house opened and her mom came out to the dog lot.

Robyn's heart sank. "Did Mr. Sterns call?"

"No. I just wanted to check with you before you take off. What should I do if he comes while you're out?"

Robyn checked her relief and considered her mother's situation. "If he doesn't call in the next hour, Rick and I are going to head out. We should be back in a couple of hours though."

"Yes, but I don't want to be here alone when he comes."

When it came down to it, Robyn didn't blame her. She'd feel the same way. "Maybe you can try to call him when we're ready to leave and see what he says."

Mom went back into the house.

Robyn laid out harnesses for four dogs each for her and Rick and got out both lightweight sleds. She decided to give Rick the newer one, as the old one was more fragile. And she would give him four strong but calm dogs. She would take four of her client's dogs herself.

Rick called promptly at eight, and she found herself grinning as she answered her phone. "Come on over. I'm good to go."

"Sterns hasn't contacted you yet?" he asked.

"Nope, and I've got the sleds out."

"I'll be there in ten minutes."

She went into the house. Mom wasn't due to go to work until one o'clock, and Robyn found her in the kitchen.

"Thought I'd bake apple crisp and take some to Grandpa tomorrow."

"Good idea. I bet he'd like some licorice, too."

Mom smiled. "Don't know how he can stand that stuff, but I'll pick some up this afternoon." She jotted it on the shopping list that hung on the refrigerator door.

"I've got to put in another order for meat for the dogs," Robyn said, watching her face.

"Okay." Neither of them spoke of how close they were cutting their finances.

When the race is over, Robyn told herself, *we should be okay for a while.*

More than two weeks still lay between them and the Fire & Ice, and all the entry fees were in the bank. They never spent any of the money from the race for anything other than race expenses until the event was over, but usually they made a profit of a couple thousand dollars.

"So, Rick's on his way over," Robyn said. "Do you want me to try to call Mr. Sterns?"

"I guess I can do it."

"Okay. If he's on his way, of course we'll stay."

Mom took her phone off the counter and pushed a few buttons. "I'm getting his voice mail." She waited a moment then said in her best "leave a message" voice, "This is Cheryl Holland. We just wondered if you planned to come up to Holland Kennel today or not. Please let us know. Thank you very much."

She closed the connection and gulped.

Robyn walked over and kissed her cheek. "Thanks. You did great."

She went out to the dog lot, and Rick soon joined her. His first words were, "Did you get ahold of Sterns?"

Robyn shook her head. "We haven't heard a word from him. Mom called his cell phone, but he didn't answer."

"Well, cell service is spotty at best outside Anchorage."

She nodded. "So, are you ready to mush?"

He grinned. "I am so ready. Who's on my team?"

"I'm letting you take Max. He's your leader. And Bandit, Dolly, and Spark."

"Who do you get?"

She picked up the first set of harness. "Oh, I'm taking four of Pat Isherwood's dogs."

"He's the guy who had the appendectomy?"

"Yes. He's paying me good money to keep them in shape for him. I try to take all eight of his dogs out two or three times a week. This past week has been tough though. I took the other half of his team out Monday, but they'll need to go again tomorrow, and no excuses."

Putting the dogs in harness with Rick helping her was an interesting experience. Despite the cold temperatures—only ten degrees this morning—Robyn found herself blushing when their faces came close together as they bent over the same dog. She'd always been independent, even more so since her brother left home. She lived in a fairly remote location and had braced herself long ago for the possibility that she wouldn't find a husband out here.

Although more men than women lived in Alaska, she'd increased the odds against finding a match by choosing not to go to college. Instead, she'd stayed home and worked in the dog business. That seemed most practical after her father died, and she loved dogs and sledding. She knew she wanted to continue Grandpa Steve's kennel business, and her mother had reluctantly agreed. But in taking that path, she had isolated herself to some extent. Her contacts were mostly through business and church now, and she'd decided not to worry about it.

"Hey, you really do know what you're doing." She laughed and straightened as Rick adjusted the harness on Bandit. "Go ahead and get Max. I'll start getting my team hitched up."

The last thing on her checklist was to alert her mom. Rather than leaving the team while she trudged to the house, Robyn called her on the cell phone.

"Are you two leaving now?" Mom asked.

"Yep, we're all set. I don't know if you'll be able to get me when we leave here, but if you do hear anything, try to give me a call."

"I will. Be safe, honey."

Robyn laughed. "Well, I've got a doctor with me, just in case."

Rick laughed, too, as she put her phone away and zipped the pocket. "You're sassy this morning."

"I feel good. Don't you? New snow, terrific dogs. . ."

"Great company," he finished.

She felt her cheeks warming again and untied the snub line for her team. Ignoring his flirtatious smile, she stepped onto the runners of her sled. "Ready?"

Rick nodded as he stowed his own line.

Robyn turned forward. "Hike!"

&

Rick couldn't remember when he'd had a better time. Robyn led him first over trails he knew well, but then they veered onto land he'd never traveled. They stopped every time the race trail changed course, or any place a hazard occurred, like a sharp drop-off or rocks hidden beneath the snow. Robyn had packed different colored ribbons for marking the way and warning signals. Their brief stops gave the dogs short rests.

Rick had thought he was in good shape, but keeping up with Robyn challenged him. He watched her jump off frequently and run behind her sled, amazed at her energy.

"Hey, watch your team," Robyn called at a stop an hour into their trek.

Rick had forgotten to set his snow hook. The minute he stepped off the runners, the dogs had leaned forward, ready to take off. "Whoa!" He jumped back onto the sled, putting his weight on the runners and reaching for the snow hook.

Robyn laughed. "Don't bother. I'll get this one. It won't take a minute." True to her word, she quickly positioned the markers where the trail took a turn and regained her position behind her team.

At the next stop, Rick was determined to prove he wasn't an absolute greenhorn. He set his hook and made sure the lines were taut before letting go of the sled.

"Not bad." Robyn tossed him a roll of plastic ribbon. "I want to mark this curve because of the rocks there. If someone runs into them, it's bad news. We've had more than one sled wreck at this spot."

Since no trees grew nearby, he held stakes she had set in the snow while she packed more of it tightly around them. "We'll need to have someone check them the day before the race," she said. "I get volunteers to run short stretches of the route that day until the whole trail is covered. It breaks the trail if we've had new snow and gives us the assurance that all the markers are still in place." She clumped the snow tightly around the last stake. "There."

Rick stood when she did. "This is fantastic. Thanks so much for letting me go with you."

She smiled up at him. "I'm having fun."

Her rich brown eyes sent him a message that made him believe she really was enjoying this morning as much as he was. He thought he knew her well enough now to interpret her moods. Had things gone beyond friendship?

Her glowing cheeks and bright eyes drew him. Now might be the time to kiss her. Or would that be too forward? He'd known her a year, but they'd spent only a little time together, most of it in the past week. He wanted to let her know how he felt—but did he really understand that himself?

He liked everything he knew about her, and each new revelation confirmed his impressions of her character. She was diligent and loyal. She loved the Lord. She cared deeply about her family, its heritage, and its well-being. And she was very pretty. But there was still so much to learn. If he told her now what he thought, would he regret it?

He leaned toward her, his heart pounding. As he reached for her, she sobered and hesitantly raised her arms. He pulled her closer. Robyn came into his arms but turned her face away, resting her head against his shoulder. His heart tumbled. Did she do that to avoid a kiss? Maybe it was too soon. But she stayed in his embrace for a moment.

Then she laughed, a sudden, contented burble.

He pulled away and eyed her cautiously.

"I'm sorry. It's not funny, but. . ." She tossed her head, her lips curved in amusement.

He tried not to let his apprehension come through in his voice. "What?"

"It just hit me how hard it is to hug someone in January

gear in Alaska." She smiled up at him. Something about her expression told him she'd found the experience enjoyable.

He nodded. "We may have to repeat this experiment when we're in a warmer place."

Her smile widened. "We'd probably better head back, in case Mom's got company." She pulled out her phone and checked it. "Just as I thought. No service out here."

"Let's go." Rick hurried to the back of his sled and reached for the snow hook. She hadn't protested his comment. As they took the trail back, he found himself looking forward to kissing her and hoping that time came soon.

The dogs pulled them back toward the Holland Kennel yard at a smart trot. Rick believed those on his towline could have kept going all day and loved it. As the miles flew by, his thoughts drifted back to their embrace. Robyn was right—parkas weren't the best attire for courting.

Cheryl came out the back door of the house as they came to a halt and ran to where Robyn hitched her team leaders. "I'm so glad you're back!"

"What is it, Mom? Did Mr. Sterns show up here?"

"Not yet, but six of our dogs are missing."

seven

"Six dogs? What do you mean?" Robyn couldn't process what her mother told her.

"I've called the police. I didn't know what else to do." Mom wrapped her arms around herself and shivered. "I don't know how this could have happened. I'm sorry."

Robyn put her arm around her mother. "You're freezing. Go inside. We'll put the dogs away and come right in."

Rick had tied his team with a snub line and walked slowly along the yard, looking at the ground. "These look like fresh snow machine tracks," he called.

"Yes, they were pulling a trailer with a box or cage on it." Mom's eyes swam with tears. "I would have heard them, but after Mr. Sterns called, I decided to do some vacuuming, and when I shut it off, I heard the motor out here, but it was too late. By the time I got to the window, they were already pulling out."

"Wait," Robyn said. "Sterns called you?"

"Yes. About twenty minutes after you left. He told me he'd come around noon. I tried to get you, but I couldn't get through, so I started cleaning up the house. I decided it was a good time to. . .well, that doesn't matter. The thing is, when I heard the motor and ran to the kitchen window, I saw this snow machine with a trailer leaving the yard and going out that old woods road. I figured someone had just driven through, even though we have it posted not to. I was a little mad, but it happens."

Rick had come over and stood beside Robyn, listening.

Mom went on, "Then I saw that one gate was open."

Robyn swung around and looked at the enclosures. "Both

76

gates are closed now."

"Because I shut the one to the male dogs' yard. It was wide open. I knew you wouldn't leave it that way, so I ran out to look. Tumble was gone. And you'd said you were taking some of Pat Isherwood's dogs out this morning, so I knew that meant you didn't take Tumble for your leader."

"Right," Robyn said. "And Rick had Max leading."

Her mother nodded and her face crumpled. "When you called me right before you left, I looked out and saw that you each had four dogs in your team. I had wondered if you would take Tumble in case Sterns came while you were gone, to make sure he didn't try to take him, but I could see that you didn't. So I ran through the lot to see what other dogs were gone. I counted fourteen missing, so besides the eight you had out, it looks like six were stolen."

Rick reached out and touched her shoulder. "When will the state police be here?"

"Any time now."

"Sounds like you did the right thing. Why don't you go in and put the kettle on? Robyn and I will take care of the teams and be in shortly."

She nodded, and her face quivered. "I feel so. . .angry. Angry and stupid."

"Don't," Robyn said softly. "We'll get them back." She wished she believed that.

Her mother turned and trotted toward the house.

Robyn looked at Rick. "What do you think?"

"It's very odd. Sterns calls and says he won't come around for three hours or more, and then thieves come into the lot in broad daylight and steal six dogs."

Robyn nodded. "Yes, including Tumble, the dog he was so angry about not getting. Let's put these mutts away and make a list of who's missing."

They quickly stripped off the dogs' harnesses and piled them on Robyn's sled. When all of the dogs they'd exercised were tethered to their kennels, Robyn walked around the lot. She'd already realized the six missing dogs included two of Patrick Isherwood's team, Wocket and Astro. Tumble and three other Holland Kennel dogs had also been taken.

"Odd," she said, looking over the female dogs' enclosure. "If it was Sterns, why didn't he take the three females he wanted to buy?"

"Better yet, why didn't he take *any* females?"

"Hmm." Robyn looked back toward the other side of the lot. "Maybe they didn't want to waste time. If he knew he wanted Tumble, he'd go for him first and grab whichever other dogs were closest. That way he could get in and out quick."

"Do you think they watched us leave?"

"Maybe. And maybe they didn't realize Mom was in the house. You'd think they'd have heard the vacuum, but not if they waited back in the woods; and when they came out, their own motor would drown it out."

The reality hit her, and she pressed her hands against her churning stomach. "This rots."

Rick came over and stood in front of her. She couldn't help looking up into his sympathetic eyes. In today's cold sunshine, they were the color of swirled caramel. At any other moment, she'd have pondered the embrace they'd shared on the trail, and how she was sure Rick would have kissed her if she'd encouraged him. But she couldn't think about it now. Not with Tumble and five other dogs hijacked out of her lot. "What am I going to tell Patrick?"

Rick gritted his teeth. "The truth. I'd wait until the officer gets here though. See what he thinks your chances are of recovering the dogs. Then give Patrick a call and tell him exactly what happened."

Rick stood by while Cheryl and Robyn talked to the trooper, Officer Glade, in their living room. He wished he could do more, but both women assured him they valued his support.

"This is all the information I have about Philip Sterns." Cheryl handed Glade the sheet of paper on which she'd carefully listed Sterns's name, phone number, and the hotel where he'd stayed in Anchorage. Robyn was able to add the license plate number of his rental car.

"Are you certain it was Sterns who came here today and took the dogs?" Glade asked.

"No, not at all." Cheryl spread her hands helplessly. "He's the only one I could think of. He'd expressed interest in our stud dog, Tumble, and he was angry when Robyn and Steve said they wouldn't sell him. I can't help thinking he may have decided to just take what he wanted."

Glade took a few notes.

Robyn hauled in a deep breath. "But, Mom, he didn't take the other three dogs he wanted." She turned to the trooper. "Mr. Sterns wanted to buy the one male—that's Tumble—and three breeding females. But the six dogs that were stolen were all males. If he really wanted to start a breeding kennel, why take six males?"

Rick thought that was an excellent question. Of course, Sterns may have simply been in too much of a hurry to be choosy, but as Robyn had told him earlier, he knew exactly where Coco and the other dogs he'd picked out were tethered.

"Was the dog yard locked?"

Robyn shook her head. "We lock the gates every night, but since it was daytime and Mom was here, I didn't bother this morning. I latched them securely after we took the team dogs out, but no locks."

Rick stepped toward Glade. "Officer, I did a little investigating on Robyn's behalf yesterday. She'd told me about the situation with this potential buyer. I have a friend in the police department—perhaps you know him. Joel Dawes."

"Sure, I know Dawes." Glade eyed Rick with new speculation. "You talked to him about this business?"

Rick hoped Joel hadn't done anything beyond his clear-cut duty in helping him. No way to get out of telling the trooper now though. "I asked him to do a quick check on Sterns, and he did. He found out the man has a criminal record in California. In fact, he's spent some time in the California Correctional Center."

"All right," Glade said. "I'm going to my vehicle and call this in. We need someone in Anchorage to contact his hotel and see if he's checked out. If he has, we can find out fairly easily whether he's left Alaska. It shouldn't be too hard to find a man traveling with six dogs."

"Is there anything else we can do?" Cheryl asked.

"Just stay calm. After I call this in, perhaps Miss Holland could show me the kennels and the snow machine tracks. I may be able to tell whether they were waiting for you and Dr. Baker to leave this morning."

Rick nodded, glad he hadn't followed the tracks on impulse. He might have ruined some evidence.

"We'll put our boots and coats on," Robyn said. "Whenever you're ready, just come and tell us."

Glade went out to his car, and Cheryl went to the kitchen to start a pot of coffee.

Rick took Robyn's hand and drew her toward the sofa. "Come here for a minute. I wondered if you'd like to pray about this together."

The cloud lifted from her face. "Thank you. I'd like that a lot."

They sat down, and Rick bowed his head. He wished he had the perfect words to say, the ideal way to make things better for Robyn, but all he could do was pour out his heart. "Lord, thank You for sending Trooper Glade out. You know where those dogs are and who is responsible for this. I ask now that You'd keep them safe and comfort Robyn and Cheryl. If it's in Your plan, please let the thieves be caught and the dogs returned."

He didn't expect Robyn to pray, too, but when he said, "Amen," she said softly, "Lord, please keep the dogs safe and let us get them back. Especially Pat's dogs. Thank You."

She squeezed his hand and released it. He opened his eyes. Her smile was a bit wobbly, but she seemed calmer.

They stood, and Rick glanced out the window. Glade was getting out of his truck. Beyond his vehicle, an SUV turned in from the road.

Rick caught his breath. "Robyn?"

"Yeah?"

"Isn't that—"

"I don't believe it." She turned toward the kitchen door. "Mom! Come in here quick! Philip Sterns just drove in."

❧

"Either he's got a lot of nerve, or he's innocent." Mom stood between Robyn and Rick, peering out the front window.

"Should we go out?" Robyn felt as though she was watching a crime drama through the glass.

"It looks like Trooper Glade is going to ask him a few questions," Rick said.

Robyn looked up at him and scowled. "I don't know about you two, but I want to hear what he says."

Rick chuckled. "What do you say, Cheryl? Shall we join them?"

Mom was already pulling on her jacket. The three of them walked out to the driveway together.

"Mrs. Holland! Robyn!" Sterns's mouth drooped as they approached. "The officer just told me what happened. I'm so sorry."

Robyn decided to keep her mouth shut. If she voiced her thoughts right now, it wouldn't be pretty, and it might compromise the trooper's investigation. Mom, however, stepped forward with a regretful smile.

"Thank you, Mr. Sterns. At least the three dogs you spoke for weren't taken."

"Oh? I'm glad to hear that. I assume you still want to do business? I came ready to pay for them and take them with me." He took out his wallet.

Mom turned and said to Robyn, "You want to go ahead with this, don't you?"

Robyn wished she could have more time to think about it. Since her roster of female dogs had not been depleted, she supposed it was all right—if Sterns wasn't behind the theft.

"I. . .guess so." She reached out and took the money, knowing that sealed the bargain. "I'll get you a receipt."

"I've got cages in the vehicle. Should I drive around back to the dog yard?" Sterns asked.

Trooper Glade said, "I'd rather you didn't do that, sir. I'm not done looking at the evidence out there."

Cheryl said, "Is it all right for my daughter to go into the female dogs' enclosure and bring out the three dogs this gentleman is buying?"

"I suppose so," Glade said. "While you do that, I'd like to ask Mr. Sterns a few more questions."

"Of course. And if you'd like, you can talk inside. It's quite chilly out here." Mom arched her eyebrows and Sterns nodded.

"Thank you," Glade said. "Perhaps that's best."

Sterns held out his key ring to Robyn. "The cages are in the back of my rental."

"I'll help you," Rick said.

Robyn felt immense relief. Selling a dog always saddened her, but under the circumstances, she was afraid she might break down and cry. That or say something she'd regret later. "Thanks."

Together they walked around the house, while Mom took Glade and Sterns inside.

"Are you okay?" Rick asked.

She puffed out a breath of cold air. "As well as can be expected, I guess."

"I know what you mean." He shook his head as she unfastened the door to the shed. "I don't like it."

Robyn reached inside and grabbed three leashes off the hook near the door. She handed him one. "Me either. Based on what little we know right now, I still think Sterns is behind this mess. But without proof, I couldn't see a good reason to call off the deal."

She clipped her leash to Coco's collar then unhooked her tether line. Holding the end of the leash firmly, she knelt beside the dog she and Grandpa had raised from a pup and hugged her. "Bye, girl," she whispered. "I hope he's good to you."

Coco whined and licked her face. Robyn felt tears welling in her eyes and knew there was no sense prolonging the moment. She rose and handed the end of the leash to Rick. "Can you take her, please? I'll get Rosie."

He waited while she repeated the procedure with the second dog. When she stood, he smiled mournfully. "Is it always this hard?"

"Sort of. But I usually don't think I'm handing them over to a thief. We make sure they'll have a good home."

"And you're not sure this time."

She shrugged helplessly. "The setup Sterns described sounds terrific. . .assuming he's telling us the truth. But if I refuse to let them go now. . ."

Rick nodded. "He could get really nasty, I suppose. But if you want to say no, I'll stand behind you."

Her mouth skewed into an involuntary grimace and she looked away. "I can't ask you to take the heat for me. And you have patients to see this afternoon. You can't stay around and guard Mom and me if we make him mad."

"You could announce it while the state trooper's here. I'd think that would deter Sterns from doing anything rash."

She bit her bottom lip and considered that. "Thanks. I appreciate everything you're doing today. Just having you here is a big help. But I think right now we should smooth things over. I don't want to put Mom in a situation that's worse than the one we've got right now. And besides—" She hesitated, but looking up into his caramel-colored eyes and seeing the sympathy he radiated, she knew she could tell him anything. "We really need the money."

"I thought maybe. But I hate to see you do something you don't want to do." Rick sighed then pulled out a smile. "Okay, I'll support your decision. Robyn, I care about you and your family. I'll do anything I can to help you."

She tried to smile, but her lips trembled too much. A fresh memory of his awkward embrace on the trail sent a dart of yearning to her heart. The possibility that Rick liked her beyond their casual friendship delighted her, but she couldn't spare the time to think about that now. Instead, she sniffed and got out a muffled, "Thanks."

Rick's smile twisted as though her pain had reached him, too. "You want to get the last dog, and we'll take them out to Sterns's vehicle?"

When all three dogs were loaded in the cages in the back of the rented SUV, they went inside. Mom sat on the edge of Grandpa's recliner in the living room and smiled wanly when Robyn and Rick came in.

Robyn cocked her head and listened. The two men were talking in the kitchen.

"I gave them coffee and left them alone," Mom said, rising. "I suppose I should get ready for work."

Robyn went to the desk in the corner and found her receipt book. She hesitated only a moment then wrote out the document for Philip Sterns. She crossed the living room and stood in the doorway. "The dogs are loaded, Mr. Sterns."

He turned around to smile at her, and she handed him the receipt. "Thank you. Officer Glade and I were just discussing the incident that took place here earlier. I want to tell you personally, I had nothing whatever to do with this. I hope you don't think otherwise."

Robyn found it hard to meet his gaze. "Right now we're still in shock. We don't know what to think."

"I guess you can go, Mr. Sterns." Glade closed his notebook and stood.

"I assure you, I'm happy to cooperate," Sterns told him. "It's a shame someone stole that beautiful dog, Tumble. If there's anything else I can help you with, I'll be happy to do it."

Glade nodded and looked at Robyn. "I'm going out to look at the tracks now. Can I go out this door?" He glanced toward the back door that led into the dog lot.

"Yes. Would you like me to come out with you?"

"I'll go take a look. Maybe you can step out after you've seen Mr. Sterns off and show me where each of the stolen dogs was kept."

When the door closed behind him, Robyn faced Sterns. "Have you booked passage for the dogs to California?"

"Actually, they're staying here in Alaska."

Robyn couldn't hide her surprise, and he smiled. "I've found some property outside Anchorage. I'll board the dogs at a kennel near the city while I go back to California to wind up my affairs there. I'm returning in two weeks to close on the house I'm buying. Unless, of course, you and your grandfather have changed your minds about selling this place."

"No, thank you. I hope the dogs will be happy with you and that you have good times together."

"That's gracious of you. Perhaps we'll see you at some race or other." He walked through the living room, said good-bye to Rick, and went out to his car.

Robyn drew a deep breath and let it out slowly.

"You holding up all right?" Rick asked.

"Kind of."

Her mother entered the room from the hallway that led to their bedrooms. "At least that's over," Mom said. "What are we going to do about Pat Isherwood's dogs?"

"After I show Trooper Glade what he needs to see, I'll call Pat. I can't put it off."

"I suppose not. Well, I don't have time to eat lunch. I need to get to the store."

"I'm not sure I can eat anyway," Robyn said. "Want me to make you a sandwich to take with you?"

"No, that's all right." Cheryl turned to Rick. "I'm so glad you were here when this happened, and when Mr. Sterns came. I admit I was a little frightened to see him again."

"I'm glad I could help," Rick said. "Robyn, do you mind if I go out to the kennels with you?"

"Not at all. Thanks."

Glade came slowly along the path from the old woods road, studying the snowmobile's trail as they walked across the yard.

Robyn smiled grimly as they met near the dog enclosures. "This is the female dogs' enclosure. No dogs were taken from here, though the three Sterns just bought were all in here. When Mom told us about the theft, I looked around a little. Of course, we had to put away the teams we'd taken out. I couldn't tell for sure, but I don't think the thieves came into this enclosure."

Glade nodded, still searching the ground. "It looks to me as if they stopped the snow machine over there." He pointed to the other gate. "And I'd say there were two of them, though Mrs. Holland didn't specify she saw two people. But she was looking at the back of the rig, with the trailer between her and the snow machine."

"True," Robyn said. "I'm sorry we messed up the footprints and all."

"Well, you couldn't leave your teams out, I suppose."

"I didn't go too close to the kennels where the six dogs were stolen on purpose. I thought you might want to look over the ground for evidence. I'll take you in there now if you want."

The dogs began to yip as she opened the gate. "Shush," Robyn called, and for the most part, they did.

Rick and Glade followed her into the male dogs' enclosure.

The dogs that hadn't been out for exercise that morning jumped and whined as she passed them. Tumble's absence struck her suddenly with the force of a meteorite. His tether line lay slack on the snow, and his kennel sat empty and silent. A painful lump rose in her throat. "Tumble was here."

"He's your best dog?" Glade asked.

She nodded. "He's our primary stud dog. We sell the pups and collect stud fees. And he's a terrific leader, too."

"How much is he worth?"

She put her hand to her lips and blinked back tears. Would it come down to this—placing a number on Tumble's life for the police and the insurance company? "I. . .let me think." She named a figure and shrugged. "Maybe more. But that's taking into account what he could earn for us and the prestige his record brings to the kennel."

Glade wrote it down and studied the ground around Tumble's doghouse. The thief's footprints were indistinguishable from Robyn's on the packed snow.

She showed him the next empty kennel. "This dog belonged to a client, and so did the one beside him. I have eight of Patrick Isherwood's dogs here to train while he recovers from surgery."

"How many of the stolen dogs were his?"

"Two."

"The other four were yours?"

"Yes, sir." Robyn eyed Rick while the trooper wrote it all down. Rick's confident demeanor and sympathetic smile encouraged her a little, but the entire situation still ripped her insides to shreds.

When Glade had inspected all of the empty kennels, Rick said, "Officer, we still wonder about this Philip Sterns. The whole situation is off-kilter, with him wanting to buy dogs and getting angry over the male, then showing up today to buy the three females shortly after the others were stolen."

"I agree," Glade said, "but I don't have enough evidence to arrest him. I did get the name of the kennel where he said he would board the dogs he bought, and you can be sure we'll check into that."

"You know about the microchips, right?" Robyn asked. "For identification."

"My dog has one," the trooper said.

"Well, so do all of these dogs. We put them in our puppies and any dogs we buy that don't already have them. Patrick's dogs have them, too."

"That's good to know." He made a notation then glanced up. "Does Sterns know about them?"

"I. . ." She felt her face color. "He must. It's common knowledge. But I don't recall specifically discussing it with him. I should have, but I've been so upset about this—him wanting to buy Tumble, and now having six dogs stolen. I'm afraid I didn't say anything to him about it."

"That could work in your favor." He put his notebook away. "We'll do everything we can, Miss Holland."

"Thank you," Robyn said. "We're talking about a huge loss to the business, as I'm sure you realize."

Robyn and Rick walked around to the front of the house with him. When he'd driven away, they went inside.

Cheryl sat curled up in Steve's recliner, sobbing.

"Mom?" Robyn rushed to her side. "I thought you'd left."

"I'm sorry, honey." Mom reached for a tissue and dabbed at her eyelids. "I shouldn't have stopped long enough to think about things. I kind of lost it, I'm afraid. I know we've done everything we can, but I feel so horrid! It's my fault."

"Don't say that." Robyn sat on the arm of the chair and hugged her mom close. "If Sterns is behind this, then it's my fault if it's anyone's. I'm the one who made him mad, not you."

"But right in daylight, of all things, when we have so many dark hours they could have done it in."

"I know." Robyn rubbed her mom's back and caught Rick's eye. He gave her a sympathetic smile but looked as though he wished he were elsewhere. Robyn continued to stroke Mom's shoulder. "They probably watched the house for a few days and thought you worked every morning. If they came by the old woods road today, they'd have seen Rick and me hitching up the teams, but they couldn't see that your car was in the garage. When we left, they assumed the house was empty and they could do whatever they wanted."

"This isn't your fault, Cheryl," Rick said, "or yours either, Robyn. It's the thieves' fault. No one else's."

Robyn knew that he was right in an elemental way, but she still felt guilty and responsible.

"Do you think they'd have taken more dogs if we hadn't come back when we did?" Rick asked.

"I don't know." Robyn frowned, thinking about the possibilities.

"I upset Grandpa, too," Mom persisted. "It was stupid of me ever to mention selling the property. When Sterns talked about buying the place, it just popped into my mind as a possible solution to all our financial troubles. But it wouldn't be, really. I can see that now."

"Oh, Mom. Stop beating yourself up. I love you so much." Robyn squeezed her, feeling her mother's chest wrack with each breath that was more of a sob. "Look, do you want me to call the store and tell them you'll be late?"

Her mother sniffed and straightened. "No, I've already asked them several favors in the last week. I've got to go in today. But tomorrow we'll go to see Grandpa again, all right? Can you go with me?"

"Of course."

"I'll be at the clinic tomorrow," Rick said. "If it's any help, I could drive you ladies to Anchorage with me. If you want to stay in town all day, that is."

Mom wiped her face and glanced in the mirror near the front door. "Ick. I'm a mess. Rick, thank you. Why don't you settle that with Robyn? If she thinks it would be inconvenient, we'll take the car. Now, I've got to run." She bustled out the door, wiping her eyes with the tissue.

Rick glanced at his watch. "I'd better get going, too. I need to drive to a farm on the Palmer Road. Will you be all right?"

"I suppose so. I locked all the gates when we came out of the yard. You can bet I'll never leave them unlocked again, even when I'm right here in the house."

Rick paused, looking down at her, and she suddenly remembered again the hug he'd given her while their dog teams waited on the trail. Her cheeks went hot. In spite of all that had happened in the last two hours, the affinity between them mushroomed to occupy almost all her thoughts.

And yet, she wondered if she ought to let her feelings go too far down that trail. Rick still commuted to Anchorage. Would he give up his small-town practice and go back to the larger clinic? Just because he was helping her now didn't mean he would always be around.

"I'll call you later," he said softly. "And I'll be praying that the police find the dogs. Think about whether you want to ride with me tomorrow. I'll leave around eight."

"Thanks."

He reached out and rubbed his knuckles gently over her cheek. "It's going to be okay."

She nodded.

He went out quickly and closed the door.

She stepped to the window and watched him get in his truck and drive away. Her heart longed to be with him. Would his attention last?

Other things vied for her concentration. More than anything, she dreaded calling Patrick, but she couldn't put it off. Sending up a quick prayer, she pulled out her phone.

eight

That evening, Rick drove to the little church Cheryl had told him the Holland family attended. He didn't know if they would be there tonight—after today's events, going out for the midweek Bible study and prayer time would take an effort of the will. But maybe that was best. Without Robyn there to distract him, he might have a clearer mind and make a better assessment of the church.

Three dozen people sat in small groups, sprinkled about the auditorium, talking softly. Rick spotted Robyn and her mother almost at once, in the fourth row. The leap his heart took surprised him a little.

He paused near the door for a moment before walking down the aisle. He couldn't slip into a seat near the back and let her find out later he'd come in without speaking to them. But would she welcome his presence?

That was silly. Of course she would. But was she ready to let her fellow church members see him single her out?

He walked hesitantly down the aisle.

"Well, hi, Dr. Baker." A man whose cattle he treated regularly stood and shook his hand. "Glad to see you here."

"Thanks. Thought I'd visit and check it out." Rick felt foolish but quickly reminded himself of his purpose.

"You're welcome any time."

He nodded and moved away, hoping he'd conversed long enough to be polite. The service would start any minute, and he didn't want to be caught standing in the aisle.

Robyn looked up when he paused at the end of her pew. "Hi."

She smiled and moved over. "Did you see all your patients this afternoon?"

"Yes." He settled beside her and whispered, "I wasn't sure if you'd be here, but I wanted to visit this church. The Lord's helping me arrange things to spend less time in Anchorage, and I've asked Him to show me a place to worship near home, too."

"That's great. I hope you like it here."

Cheryl grinned at him. "Hi, Rick."

He smiled back and faced the front as the pastor moved to the lectern.

Rick was very conscious of Robyn sitting beside him during the Bible study. She listened intently and found her way around her Bible with ease. And she smelled great.

After a while, he was able to rein in his thoughts and concentrate on the pastor's words. He found himself liking the man and the message, which came directly from Romans chapter 10.

When the time to give prayer requests came, the pastor said, "The Hollands have asked for prayer for Grandpa Steve and also for their business. They had an incident this morning at the kennel, and six of their dogs were stolen. The police are working on it, but pray that the dogs will be found. This could make a big difference to the business, and some of the dogs were special friends. Robyn tells me two of them belonged to someone else and were here for training."

Robyn kept her head down as he gave the report. Rick wished he could encourage her. He wanted to give her hand a squeeze, at the very least.

As the pastor moved on to another request, she glanced up at him. Her dark eyes held a sheen of tears.

"You okay?" he whispered.

She nodded. "Thanks for being here. God knows where the dogs are, but. . .having you here helps."

Warmth spread through his chest. He sat back, silently giving thanks to the Lord for leading him here tonight.

The next morning, Robyn hurried to feed the dogs and get showered and changed for the trip to Anchorage. She made sure all the gates were securely locked. Even so, she hated to drive off and leave the homestead unoccupied all day.

When she was ready to go, just after eight o'clock, she joined her mother in the living room.

Mom was talking on the phone but signed off and gave her daughter a wan smile. "That was Trooper Glade. The kennel owner in Anchorage confirmed that Sterns is boarding three sled dogs with him."

"It's a reputable concern," Robyn said grudgingly. "I thought I'd heard of them, and I checked out their Web site last night. It looks like a decent place."

Her mother eyed her cautiously. "Are you sure you want to go today?"

"Yes. I haven't seen Grandpa for two days. Besides, I've got to pick up the vet logs and time sheets for the race."

"Okay. We can make the bank deposit in town, too."

"Got it right here." Robyn patted her leather shoulder bag, where the cash Sterns had given them for the dogs rested. "Let's go. I'd like to be home by suppertime if we can."

In the car, Mom drove down the Glenn Highway in silence. The sky was still dark, and the mountains were black hulks in the distance. After a while, she glanced over at Robyn. "You could have ridden into town with Rick."

"No, we needed our own wheels to do all our errands."

"You like him, don't you?"

Robyn swallowed hard and looked out the side window. What she felt for Rick had burgeoned in the past week to more than mere liking. But how could she explain that to her mother?

"I mean, we all like him," Mom persisted, "but it seemed to me yesterday that there was something a little extra between you two. And then he showed up at church last night."

"Yeah. I like him. A lot."

"That's great. He's a good man."

Robyn inhaled deeply and let her breath out in a puff. "Do you think. . .I mean, I've thought for quite a while now God might want me to be single."

Her mother laughed softly. "How long has this been going on, honey? You're only twenty-four."

"I know, but I'm not exactly in a high-circulation area. Who do I meet? The same people at church week after week, and a few dog lovers."

"Huh." Her mother shook her head, her lips pursed in an almost-smile. "I guess it would be hard for God to bring the right man for you to Wasilla."

"You know what I mean." Robyn scrunched up her face and gritted her teeth.

Mom laughed. "Yes, I do, but for the last year you've had a handsome, intelligent, single man living next door to you. Haven't you ever thought about Rick as eligible until the past week?"

"Well, sure, but. . ." Robyn turned away again, her old insecurities taking over. She'd never figured she had a chance with Rick. "I wasn't going to chase him."

"Of course not. But since the day of Grandpa's accident, he's been coming around a lot."

"Yeah." *More than he had the entire previous year*, Robyn thought. She'd first started hoping he would notice her last year, when he helped with the Fire & Ice sled race. But he was always on the go—running to Anchorage to the vet clinic or working at his own new practice down the road. She saw him only now and then, when a dog needed attention. Things had definitely changed in the last ten days.

They went to the bank first, then to the nursing home. Grandpa's face brightened when he saw them. "Hey, how you doing? My two lovely girls!"

Both kissed him and sat down to talk.

"Only a couple of weeks till the race," he said. "I gotta get out of this place."

"You're getting better," Mom said. "The nurse told me so."

"Well, they'd better let me go home before race day, or I'm going to know the reason why."

Robyn suppressed a laugh. It wasn't funny—if he couldn't go home, they *would* know the reason.

After half an hour, she stood. "I've got some errands to run, Grandpa. I'll come back for Mom in a couple of hours."

"What are you doing?"

"Picking up supplies and paperwork for the race."

"Hey, have you got all the vendors lined up?"

"Darby Zale and her mother are doing that. They've done a fantastic job, too. And Anna's got all the volunteers scheduled."

"Did you get enough people for all the checkpoints?"

"Yes, we did."

"And Rick is still going to do the vet exams at the start?"

"Yes, Grandpa. Mom can tell you who's doing what. I need to go get things done."

After quickly completing several of her errands, Robyn headed toward the newspaper office. The sun had risen, which made her feel more energetic and made it easier to find her destinations. As she nosed into yet another parking spot, her cell phone rang.

Rick's warm voice greeted her. "Hey! I guess you got to town all right?"

"Yes. I'm just going into the newspaper office. They promised us advance coverage for the race, and I brought them some information. I want them to see my face, so they won't forget about the article."

"Sounds like a plan. Say, how about lunch?"

"Together? Uh. . .you and me?"

"Yeah. Your mom's welcome, too, if she wants to come."

"Well, we were planning to eat with Grandpa at the home, but. . ."

"Of course."

Robyn sucked in a breath that seemed a little short on oxygen. "If you're serious, I'll ask them if they'd mind."

"Great. There's a place close to the nursing home. I could meet you there. I'm seeing patients until noon, but I could get over there by twelve thirty."

Robyn soon arranged the plan with her mother, who sounded thrilled that the two young people were getting together for a meal. Robyn called Rick back to tell him she'd be there.

She took her file folder into the news office and chatted for a few minutes with one of the reporters, who took notes and promised that the article would run the following week.

Leaving the office, Robyn noted that she had only a half hour before she was to meet Rick. She took out the list of Anchorage kennels she'd put together the night before, from Internet searching and the Yellow Pages. No time to visit any of them before lunch, and her stomach had begun to perform forward rolls every time she thought about seeing Rick again. On a lunch date. Deep breaths.

She got to the restaurant before he did. After looking around the parking lot to make sure he wasn't there, she walked to the shop next door and asked if she could hang a flyer for the race in their window, where other events were posted. The icy cold glass tingled her fingers as she taped up the flyer.

She got back to the restaurant as Rick parked his pickup. He climbed out and grinned when he saw her near the entrance. Suddenly Anchorage in January felt like a tropical beach. Robyn was sure her face turned scarlet.

The restaurant was full, but they waited only a few minutes before a table opened for them.

"Get your errands done?" Rick asked after they'd given their orders to the waitress.

"Yes, mostly. I need to pick up the trophies, but the shop

is near the highway, so I think Mom and I will stop there on our way home."

"Everything's coming together for the race, then."

"Yes." She frowned, feeling she must have overlooked something. "Every year it rushes up at us, and we have a thousand details to take care of, then suddenly it's over."

"Sounds about right. Have you thought about security?"

"Quite a lot since yesterday. We decided to hire someone to watch the dog lot that day."

"Too bad it had to come to that."

"I know, but if we go off all day and leave the place unprotected. . .and the whole world will know we're over at the race."

"Are you taking any dogs?"

"I usually have a few of our best ones hitched up and showing off at the race to advertise. Darby and my brother, Aven, will be helping." She clenched her jaw for a moment. "Of course, Tumble was going to be our poster child for the kennel. If we don't get him back. . .oh Rick, I'm so discouraged."

"I guess it's hard not to be."

"The police don't have any leads yet, or if they do, they haven't told us. Mom talked to Trooper Glade this morning, and all he did was assure her that Sterns actually took the dogs he bought to the kennel he said he'd use." She looked up as the waitress appeared with their plates. After the woman had set them down, Robyn smiled across the table. "Would you like to ask the blessing?"

"Sure."

After he'd prayed, they began to eat, and Robyn steered the conversation to his work. She enjoyed hearing about the four-footed patients he'd treated that morning.

"It's been awhile since I examined a ferret," Rick concluded. "And a woman brought in the most beautiful Persian kittens."

They ate for a few minutes. He took a sip from his coffee and set the cup down. "Hey, things are going to be okay. You know that, don't you?"

"Thanks. I admit I'm still fretting over the dogs. Especially Tumble and Pat's two dogs."

"We'll keep praying," Rick said.

Robyn ate the last bite of her sandwich and opened her bag. As she took out a piece of paper, the waitress approached.

"Dessert, folks?"

Rick raised his eyebrows and smiled at her. "Piece of pie?"

"No thanks, but you go ahead if you want."

"No, we're all set," Rick told the waitress. She totaled the bill and laid it on the table. "So what's that?" Rick nodded toward the paper Robyn had unfolded.

"It's a list of kennels in the area. I want to go by that place where Sterns left Coco and the other two dogs."

"Why? The police said it was legit, and I mentioned it to Hap Shelley this morning. He says the couple who own the place are honest and treat the animals well."

Robyn frowned. "Call me stubborn if you want, but I'd like to see it for myself."

"Okay, Stubborn. But let me go with you."

"Can you do that? I thought you had to get back to the clinic."

"It's not far from here." He looked at his watch. "Plenty of time."

She left her car in the restaurant's lot and climbed into Rick's pickup with him. She was surprised when, just a few minutes later, they entered a residential area and pulled in at a house with a kennel sign out front.

Following signs, they walked around the house. A din of yapping erupted, and several dogs in fenced runs leaped up and barked at them.

A woman met them just inside the entrance. "May I help you?"

Robyn cleared her throat. "Yes, I'm Robyn Holland, and I'd like—"

"Of the Holland Kennel in Wasilla?"

"Yes." Robyn stared at her.

The woman smiled. "One of my clients recently bought some dogs from you. They're beautiful."

"Why, thank you. That's why we're here, actually." Robyn peered toward the door that led to the kennels and dog runs.

"Did you. . .want to see the dogs?" The woman frowned.

Rick stepped forward. "We just wanted to inquire, since we were in town, and make sure they'd arrived safely and are adjusting well."

She nodded, eyeing him thoughtfully. "Have we met?"

"I'm Dr. Rick Baker, from the Far North Veterinary Hospital."

"Of course." Her expression cleared.

"Miss Holland is extremely particular about making sure the dogs she sells are well cared for," he said. "I told her this is one of the top kennels in Anchorage."

"Thank you. I can assure you the dogs are all fine. They seem to be settling in well. Mr. Sterns expects them to be here for a couple of weeks."

Robyn nodded. Probably the woman had security rules that wouldn't let just anyone walk in and visit dogs that belonged to other people.

"I. . .I also wondered if you'd had any other dogs come in yesterday or today that might be. . ." She looked down at the floor, unsure how to proceed.

The woman said carefully, "The police were here this morning, looking for stolen dogs."

Robyn nodded, attempting to hold back tears that sprang into her eyes. "We had six dogs stolen."

"I'm so sorry. We've only had two others check in within the last twenty-four hours, and they're both repeat clients. But if anyone shows up with several well-cared-for huskies,

I'll let the police know."

"Thank you." Robyn pulled the list of kennels from her bag. "Could you please tell me what you know about these places? I thought perhaps we should call them and ask if anyone had brought dogs in. . . ."

The woman took the paper and studied it. "I know these folks, at the Aspen Kennel. That's a good one. And I think Bristol is all right. This one. . ." She touched one name and glanced into Robyn's eyes. "I don't know much about the Galloway Kennel, but what I've heard. . . ." She shook her head. "They've been in business a few years, but I wouldn't take my dog there." She ran down the list, making a few comments about each one. "This one's new, and I don't know anything about it. Never heard of this one." Finally she handed the paper back. "Sorry I couldn't be of more help."

"I appreciate it." Robyn took a card from her pocket. "Here's my card for the Holland Kennel. One of the stolen dogs was Tumble, our primary breeding male. If you hear anything—anything at all that you think might have to do with our situation—could you please call me?"

"Sure. I hope you get your dogs back." The woman pocketed the card. "Rosie is out in her run now. I think Mr. Sterns's other two dogs are inside napping. But if you step outside and look through the fence at run 4, you should see Rosie."

"Thank you." Robyn turned and went out. Rick followed her to the metal mesh fence, and she looked across the expanse, over the head of the Brittany spaniel leaping and barking at her just inches away in the first run. Sure enough, Rosie stopped trotting along the fence of her enclosure and barked at Robyn and then stood whining, her nose pushed into the mesh. Robyn clenched her shaking hands on the fence.

"We'd better go," Rick said softly.

She nodded, unable to speak. She didn't want to upset the dogs. Already, Rosie might be fretful because she'd seen her former owner. Robyn trudged to the pickup.

Rick opened the passenger door for her and offered his hand for a boost up. When he got into the driver's seat, he smiled apologetically. "Ready to go back?"

She swallowed hard. "Yeah, just take me back to my car. Thanks."

"You can tell your grandfather that these three dogs are in good hands."

She bit her lip and said nothing, but she knew she wouldn't go straight back to the nursing home.

"What's the matter?" Rick asked.

She looked up into his gentle brown eyes. "I think I'll drive over to the Galloway Kennel."

"What for?" He eyed her for a moment then reached for her hand. "No, Robyn, don't."

"What if they're over there? I can't not look. She made it sound like it's the worst kennel in town. If Tumble's in there. . ."

Rick sighed. "What's the address?"

She told him, and he started the engine.

"You're. . .taking me there?"

He said through gritted teeth, "It'll be quicker if we don't go back to the restaurant first. And I'm not letting you go alone."

nine

Almost half an hour later, they located the Galloway Kennel. Rick parked at the curb a hundred yards beyond the building.

He ought to call Far North and alert them that his lunch hour would probably stretch to two. It wasn't something he liked to do, but then, he almost never did it.

"This is a pretty bad neighborhood." He stared out at the littered sidewalk and dilapidated buildings.

Robyn raised her chin. He'd come to recognize that as a sign that she wasn't giving up. With a sigh, he got out of the truck and went around to open the passenger door for her. They went in together.

A bell on the door jingled, and a woman came from an inner room, where several dogs were barking. The warm smell of dogs and bedding met them.

"Hi," Rick said. "We're looking for some dogs that were stolen yesterday from a breeding kennel in—"

"Stolen? Why are you looking here?" The woman rested her hands on her hips and glared at them.

Rick gulped and glanced at Robyn. Wrong approach.

Robyn said, "We're contacting all the kennel owners in the area. The police are looking for these valuable dogs, but we thought perhaps business owners could help us, too. If you'd be on the lookout for—"

"Are you insinuating that we would have stolen animals here? This is outrageous."

Rick spread both hands. "No, ma'am, you don't understand. We only—"

"Oh, I understand. I understand plenty. Go on. Get out of here."

He looked at Robyn. She gritted her teeth and shrugged.

"Let's go." He reached for her arm and guided her toward the door.

When they were outside and the door shut behind them, she let out a pent-up breath. "Of all the—"

"I'm sorry." Rick walked beside her toward the pickup. "I jumped right in and said the wrong thing. I should have let you do the talking."

"Now we'll never know if they're in there."

"Maybe not. But we can ask the police to come by and take a look."

She nodded. "I guess."

Rick opened the door and helped her into the truck. Once inside, he hesitated to start the motor. "What now?"

She eyed him cautiously. "You're up for more adventure?"

"Well, I sort of feel like I'm the one who blew it." He consulted his watch. "If there's another one that's not too far from here, we could try one more. I promise to be more diplomatic this time."

"Or sneakier."

"That might work."

She smiled then. It was worth the wait, especially when she reached over and squeezed his hand. "Thanks for being here. Facing her alone would have been scary. And I do think we should ask the police to question her. As soon as possible."

Rick took his cue and pulled out his phone. He tried Trooper Glade's number. When he got no response, he rummaged in the glove box for an Anchorage street map. He handed it to Robyn, and she pored over it while he dialed his friend.

A minute later, he was able to tell Robyn, "Joel Dawes said they'll send someone out here this afternoon. I think we can count on it. And he'll let us know the outcome."

"Good." Robyn pointed to her crumpled list. "The kennel closest to this one is a new one. That lady at the first place said she didn't know anything about them. But that might be a good place to hide some hot property, don't you think?"

"Maybe so."

He drove a few miles and found the location. He and Robyn climbed out of the truck and stood by the tailgate, looking over the rundown one-story building. Paint was peeling off the siding. The front held no windows, and the door had a handwritten sign that read BARKLAND KENNEL— PICKUP HOURS 9 TO 11 A.M. AND 4 TO 6 P.M. Barking and whining came from the back of the property.

"Maybe we should let the police handle this one, too." Rick glanced hopefully at her, but her jaw was still set. "I can try Trooper Glade again. Even if they didn't come until tomorrow. . ."

"The dogs could be taken out of Alaska by then."

"Well, yes."

Her brows drew together in a scowl. "And the police aren't going to want to spend hours searching every kennel in town. I'm sure they have violent crimes that are much more urgent."

"No. They'd send someone. This is like grand theft, isn't it? Those dogs are valuable. I'm sure if I talk to Joel, I can convince him that it's important to send someone here as well as to that Galloway place."

"But if our dogs aren't here, they wouldn't go and search all the other kennels on the list."

"Is that what you plan to do?" This was getting out of hand. He'd had no idea she was so determined. No way could he blow off the clinic for the whole afternoon and escort her to half a dozen more kennels. "Robyn, I can't go around to them all with you. If I'm gone much longer, the clinic staff will send the police out to look for *me*."

The set to her mouth rebuked him. Pain and anger filled Robyn's heart right now, and it spilled over into the lines of her face and the stiff set to her shoulders. Without her saying a word, he knew she wanted to see justice done and to recover the dogs, not just for her family but for Patrick Isherwood, too.

"Did you call Pat Isherwood yesterday?" Rick asked.

"Yes."

"How did he take the news?"

She winced. "He didn't like it, of course. I assured him the other six dogs he left with us are locked in. I even asked Darby and my friend Anna to stop in today and make sure everything's okay while we're gone."

"But you feel as though you've got to find those dogs yourself, not leave it up to the state police." She didn't answer, but her stricken face roused new longings in him. He wished he could protect her from violence and crime, and beyond that, from feelings of inadequacy and failure.

"I'm going in." She stepped forward, and he grabbed the sleeve of her parka.

"Let's think about this for a minute. You know that if we walk in and ask to see the dogs, they won't let us."

"You may be right. So? Do you have a better plan?" Her dark eyes sparked with resistance.

Rick wanted more than anything to take the hurt and anger away. Not only to return the dogs to her, but to assure her that this would never happen again. It was beyond his power, but she had come to trust him, and for the last couple of days she'd relied on him in small ways. If nothing more, she might let him bear some of the stress for her.

"Let me go in and ask to see the kennel," he said. "They might recognize you."

Her puff of breath formed a white cloud in the cold air. "Or you. You were with me yesterday."

"All bundled up in a parka. Not this jacket, I might add." He patted the front of the wool jacket he'd worn to the clinic. "And they might know your face from any number of places. There's a fetching picture of you on the Holland Kennel Web site, for instance."

She blinked twice and looked away. "If you think you can distract me with flattery, forget it."

He smiled. "All right, I'll save that for later. But it's true, Robyn. They might recognize you. And have you considered that the thieves might be people you know?"

Her lips twitched. "Someone else in the dog business?"

"Maybe. Or someone in Wasilla who knows a little about your routine."

Her gaze sought his again. "So, you think we're wasting our time looking in Anchorage? What do you suggest we do?"

"Since we're here, let's go ahead and check this one. There's just one vehicle in the parking lot." He nodded toward the ten-year-old pickup sitting in front of the kennel. "Probably the owner is the only person here, or an employee. No customers right now."

"So?"

"So, what if I go in and inquire about possibly leaving a dog here for a week when I take my vacation. While I'm in there, you can sneak around the back of the building. From the sound of things, they've got some pens or tethers out there. You wouldn't be able to see any dogs that are inside, but you could at least check out the outdoor accommodations."

She nodded. "Better than nothing, I guess." She pulled her hood up and arranged it over her dark hair.

He smiled down at her. Now wasn't the time to mention it, but the image of her sweet face peering out at him from within the circle of faux fur with her brown eyes wide and her cheeks flushed stirred him. Sometime when they were in a quiet, warm place and didn't have to worry about dogs or criminals, he would tell her how lovely she was.

Had no man seen her beauty before him? It was unthinkable. But why, then, was she still single? Had her independence kept the suitors away? Perhaps her close-knit family deterred them, or her success in business intimidated them. Her seeming assurance might put off some men, he supposed, but he knew she had a wide streak of insecurity that she hid well.

Of course, he made a huge assumption there. Perhaps she had been courted and he knew nothing about it.

"I'm leaving the truck unlocked." He said it even as he made the decision. "I want you to be able to get in quickly if you need to."

She nodded. "Okay."

"Be careful," he said. "If anyone sees you, it's all right to tell them you're with me and you wanted to see the dogs. But I'm planning on you staying out of sight. I'll meet you back here in ten minutes."

"Got it," she said.

He hesitated, then bent and kissed her cool cheek. When he pulled away, she was watching him with something like curiosity in her chocolate brown eyes. Sometime he would really kiss her, and maybe that would knock the questions out of that simmering gaze.

"Go on," he said. "Get to the side of the building and give me a minute to go in and get the guy talking."

❧

Robyn tiptoed along the side of the kennel building. She ducked low beneath the small window toward the back of the wall. As she approached the rear corner, she looked back toward the street. Rick was out of sight.

She peered around the corner and saw a large, fenced enclosure. Within it, a dozen or more dogs of different sizes and breeds ran free. She couldn't see any shelter for them other than a lone pine tree that rose near the back of the lot. The dogs had no bedding to lie down on. She ducked back quickly, before they saw her. Already they were barking—one thin hound wailed continuously from a far corner and several more sporadically joined in. She hoped they weren't left out there too long in the snow with nothing to lie on.

She took another peek. Beyond the large enclosure was

another fenced area. This one seemed smaller, though it was hard to tell from her position. Inside she saw a couple of dogs that appeared to be chained to tree trunks. They lay inert on the ground. One looked like a German shepherd-husky cross. Her heart squeezed painfully. Were her dogs and Pat's in this place? She focused on the dog nearest her—a small beagle cross in the big enclosure. It was so thin she could see the outline of its ribs, and it whined without a letup. Shuddering, Robyn scrutinized the other dogs. She realized she was looking for Tumble, but if he'd been among the pitiful assortment, she'd have recognized him at once.

A loud spurt of barking erupted from inside the building, and the dogs outside took up the yapping. Some of them ran toward the back of the building and threw themselves against the fence.

She concluded that the dogs inside had begun making a ruckus because of Rick's presence, and those outside chimed in because they wanted to be part of whatever was going on. Even the ones in the far enclosure sat up and peered toward the building. Robyn decided that it no longer mattered if the dogs saw her. They couldn't possibly make more noise than they were making now.

She ran along the fence, focusing on one dog after another. None of them looked remotely like the glossy, well-fed huskies she had lost. She circled behind the pen and along the edge of the second enclosure. Her steps dragged as she realized most of the dogs within had visible injuries. Some had scabs and scars on their legs and faces. One had red lacerations on its hip, neck, and front legs. None of the wounds were covered. Looking at the hurting dogs turned her stomach and stoked the fire of her anger. She wondered if the animals out here belonged to the owner or were long-term boarders. But this was a new kennel. How had they gotten so many customers? No people in their right minds would leave pets here if they glimpsed the pitiful scene out back.

She came to the edge of the building on the side opposite where she'd started. This side held several windows. Banking that Rick would keep the owner talking in the front, she decided to take a chance and look in.

Inside, she saw a row of screened doors fronting dog cages, three deep. The animals inside yelped and whined, some pressing against the fronts of their cages. Off to her left lay an open door, and through it she glimpsed Rick standing near a desk. She quickly turned her scrutiny to the dogs in the cages. She couldn't see them well, but one particular bark, deep and insistent, rang a chord in her heart. It sounded like the bass voice of Hero, one of her largest sled dogs.

As the caged dogs moved about, she could make out their silhouettes through the mesh fencing of the enclosure doors. She stared at the cages one by one until she spotted one where the big occupant's pointed dark ears stood up above a black-and-white muzzle.

Hero!

In a flash of certainty, she knew it was him. Soon she picked out two other cages she thought likely held dogs from Holland Kennel. The others weren't within sight but could easily be on the side of the room nearer the window.

A quick look toward the open doorway made her catch her breath. Rick was backing away from the desk, nodding. As she watched, he moved out of her line of vision. She'd better head for the truck.

She glanced back toward the yard behind the building. If she took the time to go all the way around the back, Rick would be upset, wondering where she was. And the owner might look out back to see why the dogs out there hadn't settled down. She decided to chance running across the front parking lot.

Before she acted, movement inside caught her eye. She flattened herself at the edge of the window and watched a man in coveralls enter the room with all the cages. He opened one of the lower tier cage doors and clipped a leash on the occupant's collar. When he led the dog out, Robyn gasped. The husky he'd chosen was one of Pat Isherwood's lead dogs. He led it across the room and opened the back door. The dogs in the fenced yards barked and howled louder. The man came back with the leash slack in his hands.

Robyn felt sick. Had he turned Astro out with all those other dogs? What if they fought? Some sled dogs lost their manners when they met strange dogs and weren't under the owner's control. They might get aggressive—or the other dogs in the pen might. Some of the valuable huskies could be killed. The man stopped near another cage and turned his back to the window. Time to move.

She ducked low beneath the window frames and dashed to the front corner of the building. Rick stood beside the pickup, staring toward the wall where she'd begun her foray.

When she left the cover of the kennel and ran toward him, he turned, his eyes wide. She scurried to the passenger side of the truck and dove in. Rick hopped in on his side and gunned the engine.

"Wait! He's got them."

"What?" The incredulity in his expression was almost comical. His mouth hung open and his eyebrows disappeared under the lock of hair falling over his forehead.

"I saw Astro, and I'm pretty sure Hero's in there, too. He took Astro out the back. I think he put him in the pen out behind, with about twenty other dogs. They're all loose in there. Astro will probably get in a fight. They could kill him. And the worst thing is, I think he was going to put the others out there, too. Hero, especially, might get aggressive."

"Let's get down the street where he can't see us if he looks out. Then we'll decide what to do." Rick put the truck in gear and drove away. By the time Robyn had her seatbelt buckled, they were half a block down the street. "Why would he put valuable dogs in a pen with a bunch of others?" he asked.

"I don't know. Some of the dogs outside look sick and emaciated. And some of them have injuries."

"It doesn't make sense." Rick pulled in at the curb and turned to face her. "If he stole those dogs to sell, why take a chance on them getting sick or torn to pieces?"

She had no answer.

"Okay. Tell me everything."

His patience made her want to scream. "We need to call the police."

"Agreed," Rick said. "But are you sure he has them all?"

"No. He may have sold some. I think I saw two others of ours though. There are a lot of dogs in cages in the back room."

"I figured that. Heard them yelping and saw the stacked cages. It's not a good situation. I'm surprised anyone brings a dog here to board."

Robyn sucked in a deep breath. "We need to get the cops here fast."

Rick took out his phone and punched a few buttons. "Joel? This is Rick. Hey, we've located some of the stolen dogs. They're in a kennel here in Anchorage." He gave his friend the address. "We need you to send someone fast. We're afraid the dogs will be hurt. The fellow seems to be putting them together with a lot of strange dogs. Well, I don't know. I didn't see it myself, but Miss Holland did. And she's positively identified at least two of the stolen dogs, with possible IDs on two more."

Robyn tried to send him a silent message of thanks. A minute later, Rick hung up and sighed. "He says they'll need a warrant. That could take awhile."

"Can't they just come ask to take a look? Those dogs are in danger."

"Tell me exactly what you saw."

"Well, out back there are two pens. In the one I went to first, at least ten or twelve dogs were running free."

"I thought you said twenty."

She frowned. "I might have."

"Well, is it ten or twenty?"

"Yes. Somewhere in there." She looked away. "I'm sorry. I know I'm upset, but I'm not hysterical. I didn't count the dogs, okay? I'm guessing there were at least ten, possibly twenty, but no more than that. Probably twelve or fifteen."

"Okay. And how did they look?"

"Some were lethargic. Some barked constantly."

"I heard."

Robyn nodded grimly. "One at least was horribly skinny. Some of them looked okay so far as their physical conditions went. I looked them all over, and I could see right away that none of them were ours."

"What kinds of dogs?"

"Uh. . .mutts, smallish dogs. A beagle, and one that might be a coon hound. One I thought was a Scottish terrier. It's hard to tell with some of them. They haven't been groomed, and their hair is long and matted. Some mixed breeds."

"Small dogs though."

"Well. . .some. All types. I hadn't really thought about it."

Rick set his jaw firmly and checked the rearview mirror.

"So, anyway," she said, less agitated than before, "I could see that beyond it there was another fenced yard, so I walked around the perimeter of the fence. In the second pen, the dogs are tethered. There were only six or eight in there, and they weren't happy. One was chewing at the post he was hitched to. A couple were just lying in the snow. When they saw me, they barked, so I hurried around to the far side of the building, where I could hide if anyone came out the back door."

"What type of dogs in that part?"

"One looked like a husky cross. A couple of pit bulls. One I think is part German shepherd."

"So, big dogs. No little lap dogs."

"Not in that pen. And each was hitched up so they couldn't reach each other."

Rick's face had gone grim, and he focused on something far beyond the truck's windshield.

"What?" she asked.

"Just thinking."

"I could tell. Wanna share?"

He smiled but sobered almost immediately. "If they steal a top sled dog, they can't run him in races. Not in Alaska anyway. Someone who knows him would see him—because you would plaster Tumble's picture all over the place at every sled race in the state."

"I sure would. If we don't get some results today, that's exactly what I plan to do. Someone will recognize him for sure, and Hero, too, if they show up at a race."

"And they couldn't breed Tumble. How could they advertise him?"

"They could change his name."

"Yes, but it would take a couple of years for them to get any results that they could brag about. You can't just steal a breeding animal and make money by breeding him right away without revealing his identity. You have to give him time to build a new reputation. So what's the point? If they want Tumble's progeny, it would be a lot less risky to bring a good female to your kennel for breeding."

What he said made sense. Robyn held his thoughtful gaze for a long moment. "All right. So either they're going to sell them out of state, or—"

"In which case, they should have had them out of here by now, not stashed in a third-rate kennel."

"What then?"

Rick's mouth twisted as though it pained him to say the words. "What if they're planning to put them in fights?"

ten

Robyn raised her chin. "Not Tumble."

"Yes, Tumble. Hero. All of them. They took all males. Aggressive, territorial males."

She lost her assertive air and lowered her jaw, taking in a gasp of a breath. "Those dogs. . ."

"Yes?"

"The ones that were tethered."

"What about them?"

"They looked like they could have been in fights. The others, running loose in the other pen—why would they want the little ones?"

"Those might be legitimate boarders, to cover up for the illegal part of the business."

"But why would he turn Astro loose with those dogs?"

"Are you sure he turned him loose, or did he hitch him up in the other pen, where the dogs are tethered?"

She hesitated. "I don't know for sure. He came back so quickly, I assumed he'd let Astro loose. But why would he do that?"

Rick said carefully, "Maybe to see how he acted with them. To watch whether he picked a fight or not."

"You're saying they have those small breeds and mutts to. . ."

"Bait dogs. To teach the fighting dogs to go after them. Some people use cats or rabbits."

"That's awful."

"I'm not saying that's what they're doing, but it sounds like they've got one pen of smaller dogs that aren't well cared for, just waiting to be used for whatever purpose, and another pen of battle-scarred dogs that could be fighters who've been injured or are getting past their prime."

"Wouldn't they just. . .do away with them?"

Rick ran a hand over his eyes and up through his hair. "I don't know. I hear a lot of things at the clinic. It's a terrible practice, and it's illegal, but it does happen. Dog fighting, betting. And sometimes they steal pets to use as. . .training aids."

Robyn shivered. "They wouldn't do that with our dogs, would they? Valuable sled dogs?"

"More likely they're trying to replenish their fighting stock."

She shook her head. "I can't believe that. I don't *want* to believe it."

"Then don't. At least until the police tell us otherwise." He reached over and took her hand. "I'm sorry. I wish I hadn't said anything about it."

"No, that's what you were thinking and I need to know what we're dealing with. Thank God we found them today." She frowned and was silent for a moment. "When I saw the man go back inside, I thought he was going to get another dog from his cage."

"Maybe he was just going to put some of them out for some fresh air while he cleaned the cages." Rick looked back down the street behind them. He couldn't see the kennel building, but he was sure he'd see the owner's pickup if it left the parking lot. "What if I go back and take a look in those pens?"

"If he saw you, he'd recognize you. And those dogs will put up a fuss if you go near the fence."

He faced front. "True, but if I'm careful, it may be worth the risk. I just want to see if he put the rest out there, and if they're engaging with the other dogs."

As he watched her, trying to gauge her reaction, her face flushed and her muscles tensed. Tears glistened in her eyes.

Rick shook his head. "What am I saying? I know it's best if we wait for the police."

She turned quickly toward the window, shoved her hand into her jacket pocket, and pulled out a tissue.

He wasn't sure what to say or do.

"I hate this." She sobbed and held the tissue to her eyes.

Rick took a couple of deep breaths and tried to form a response that she wouldn't reject. He slid over as far as his seat would allow him and touched her shoulder. "Hey. It's going to be okay. The police are coming."

She hiccupped and wiped her face again. "Crying makes me mad."

That brought a little smile to his lips. "I can see that. You don't like feeling helpless, do you?"

She shook her head almost violently, and her hood fell back.

Rick stroked her shoulder through her padded jacket. "We've found the dogs, and we're going to get them back. All of them."

She nodded and sniffed.

"It's all right to cry a little. You've had a lot going on. Your grandpa, and the race. . ."

She sobbed again, bigger this time, and his pulse raced. Had he made things worse?

"Oh, Rick, I'm afraid that the race will be a fiasco."

"Why should it? That's silly."

"No, it's not. I've never had to host it without Grandpa. There's so much to remember. I keep thinking I'm forgetting something crucial. Will I be able to pull it off? Mom helps when she can, but her biggest contribution is putting food on the table so I don't have to worry about that and can concentrate on the business."

"The race is going to be better than ever this year."

"You're just saying that. We're talking about the family name and reputation here. The kennel's success or failure.

You know my worst fear?"

"Why don't you tell me?"

"My fear is that Mom's fears will come true. That we'll have to sell the dogs and get drudge jobs in the city." Her shoulders heaved. "With my luck, there'll be a blizzard on race day."

Rick suppressed a smile and bridged the gap between the bucket seats, pulling her head over onto his shoulder. "Shh. Stop being a gloom-and-doomer. The race will be terrific. Your brother's coming to help, remember? Your mom and I will be there. Grandpa Steve may even be able to come home to see it, even if he can't help out."

She collapsed against him, still sniffing and plying the tissue, but quieter now. He wondered if she was capable of accepting the kind of help she needed.

"You've got friends helping, too," he went on softly. "Anna and Darby and the folks over at Iditarod Headquarters."

"I do." Her small, shaky voice sounded very unlike confident, independent Robyn's voice.

"Yeah. You've got tons of friends, and a terrific roster of volunteers." He kissed her hair. "Sweetheart, it's going to be fine. You'll see." He shifted slightly on the uncomfortable edge of his seat. "Hey, look!"

Robyn sat up and followed his gaze. A police car had turned in at the end of the street and rolled toward them.

Rick opened his door and jumped from the truck, waving at the officer. "I'm Rick Baker," he told the trooper through the open car window. "I called for help about the stolen dogs."

"Trooper Straski. You've actually seen the dogs in the suspect's possession?"

"Yes, sir."

"Where is it?"

Rick straightened and pointed. "Just down there, on the right. About halfway along the block."

"Okay, we've got another officer on the way, and we've put in a request for a search warrant."

"So, will you talk to the man now?" Rick asked. "You don't have to wait for the warrant, do you? Because I'm a veterinarian, and from what we've seen, I suspect that man may be involved in a dog fighting ring."

"We'll talk to him. Where are the dogs in question?"

"Last we knew, one was in a pen behind the building with several other dogs. The rest were still caged inside. But the owner may have been transferring them all out to the pens."

"And you're the dogs' owner?"

"No, Miss Holland is. She's in my truck."

Straski glanced toward Robyn. "And what are you to Miss Holland?"

"Her neighbor. I'm Dr. Rick Baker, with Far North Veterinary Hospital." Rick figured the officer would recognize the name of the large practice, so he dropped it instead of his smaller Wasilla clinic's name.

As he'd expected, the trooper's eyes flickered. "I'm going to pull over and speak to Miss Holland."

Robyn got out of Rick's pickup and gave the trooper a shaky smile. "Thank you for coming so quickly. We're afraid those dogs are in immediate danger."

"I understand, ma'am. You're the owner?"

"Yes, I own four of the stolen dogs. Two others belonging to a client of mine were stolen yesterday as well, out of my kennel yard. Trooper Glade took all the information."

"Yes, ma'am. Can you show me your identification, please?"

Robyn looked at Rick and fumbled for her wallet. He sensed her frustration at the delay and gave her a tight smile.

When the trooper had examined her driver's license, he handed it back to her. "As soon as another officer gets here, we'll go and speak to this man. There was only one person at the kennel when you went there?"

"That's right," Rick said. "I went inside, and Miss Holland

stayed outside. She looked around the back of the building and saw the dogs in the pens."

"Some of them looked as though they'd been mistreated," she said. "Not like pampered pets that had been dropped off for care while their owners were on vacation."

A second police car approached. Rick was glad when Glade got out and walked over to join them. "Miss Holland." He touched the brim of his hat. "Dr. Baker, isn't it?"

"Yes, sir."

"Hello." Robyn's expression held genuine relief. "I'm so glad to see you again."

"I heard the call saying you'd located some stolen dogs, and I asked for the assignment."

"Thank you. They're just down there." She pointed toward the kennel and caught her breath. "Rick! Isn't that the owner's truck?"

Rick jumped to her side and looked down the street. The beat-up green pickup was pulling out of the kennel's parking lot.

≈

The green truck hadn't come more than a few yards toward them when the driver hit the brakes and backed up hastily, turning around in his parking lot. With a squeal of tires, he roared off down the street in the opposite direction.

"He saw the police cars," Robyn wailed, but the two troopers were already in motion. Glade reached his vehicle first and took off after the kennel owner. The second officer was close behind, with his strobe lights flashing.

Rick stood close beside her, watching. "They'll get him. Let's drive down to the kennel and wait there."

"All right." She'd like to be closer to the dogs. They climbed into Rick's truck, and she paused with her hand on the seatbelt's buckle. "What if some of his buddies come to the kennel while we're there alone?"

Rick shrugged. "We'll play dumb. Come on. Let's see if

any of your dogs are still there."

He turned the truck around and headed back to the kennel.

Robyn hopped out and bounded toward the door. "Locked."

She pulled a face at him, but Rick only shrugged. "When the police bring the warrant, they'll go in and get your dogs out. But they could be out back in the pens."

"That's right. Come on." She ran around the far side of the building and the length of the wall to where the fenced area began. The dogs inside started barking.

Robyn scanned the enclosure with the tethered dogs. They lunged to the ends of their chains, snapping and growling at her and Rick. Only one had the noble carriage of her huskies.

"There's Astro." She pointed. "At least he's hitched up, away from the others."

Rick studied the large Alaskan husky. A peak of black hair stuck down into the white of Astro's face, between his eyes. He strained at his chain and barked, lunging toward Robyn.

"Hush, boy," she called. "It's okay. We'll get you out of there soon."

"See any others you recognize?" Rick asked.

Robyn shook her head, wishing she could say yes. If the others had been sold or moved to another location, the police might not be able to trace them.

"Let's walk around the back and take a closer look." He held out his hand and she grasped it.

Slowly they circled the pens together and came to the side she'd first visited that afternoon. One dog paced back and forth without seeming to notice them, though several others barked continually and another lay chewing at his paw.

Rick exhaled shortly and shook his head. "They're showing signs of stress all right, and some look malnourished."

"Sad, isn't it?" Robyn hated to see animals neglected or in pain.

"I'll say. Most of them need medical care." Rick looked toward the building. "This can't be a legitimate kennel. I hate to say it, but I think my first instinct was probably right. It's a front for a fighting ring."

Robyn cringed at the thought. It meant more dogs in danger, and many maimed and killed in the past. "I hope the police catch everyone connected to this miserable outfit." She stood watching the dogs and praying silently.

"They probably shut down and move to a new spot periodically and use a different kennel name each time to make it harder for the police to catch up with them." Rick looked at his watch. "Hey, I'd better call Far North again. I should have been back over an hour ago."

"I'm sorry," Robyn said. "It's my fault."

"Don't worry about it. This is more important, and I'm sure the other vet on call can handle things and explain to the patients' owners."

He made the call, and Robyn considered calling her mother but decided to wait until she had more information. It would be wonderful to be able to tell her and Grandpa that they'd found Tumble.

About ten minutes later, Glade drove into the parking lot. "We got him. He hit a parked car, but no one was hurt, and we stopped him in an intersection. We called for backup right away. They're still untangling traffic, but I figured there were enough officers there to handle it. I wanted to make sure you knew—there are several dogs in cages in the back of that truck."

"Are the dogs all right?" Rick asked.

"We think so. One of the other troopers will drive the truck back here. Maybe you'd take a look at them, Dr. Baker."

"Sure."

Glade looked at Robyn. "And you can tell us if any of them belong to you or your client."

"Thank you. One of Mr. Isherwood's dogs is still chained

out back of this building, in a pen with some other dogs. We couldn't see any of my family's dogs or Mr. Isherwood's other one though. Will we be able to look inside the building as well?"

"As soon as the warrant gets here." Glade checked his watch. "That should be soon."

She smiled ruefully at Rick. "Again, I apologize for keeping you away from your work."

"It was worth it. We not only found out where your dogs went, but we stumbled on a lot of other dogs that need care."

"I guess I should call Mom," Robyn said. "I hoped to know more by this time, but she'll be worried if I don't check in with her soon." She took out her phone and walked a few steps away.

Her mother answered on the second ring.

"Hi, it's me," Robyn said.

"Honey, where *are* you? You can't be still with Rick."

"Yes, I am. He's right here. Mom, you'll never believe it. We found the dogs."

"What? All of them?"

"Well. . ." She gulped, wishing for a completely positive report. What if she was wrong and none of the Holland Kennel dogs were in the building or the truck? "I haven't had a close-up look at any of them yet, but we've found Astro for sure, and very likely some of the others. Maybe all of them."

"Where are they?"

"Astro is chained in a pen with some other dogs behind a crummy kennel building. We're pretty sure the others are here, too. The police are bringing a warrant to search the place, and they've arrested the guy who was running it."

"What? Slow down and tell me everything."

The green pickup, with the front fender on the passenger side crumpled and the headlight spilling shards, pulled in off the street.

"Mom, I've got to go. They have some dogs for me to look

at and see if I can identify any of ours. I'll call you later." She walked over to join Trooper Glade and Rick.

Straski brought the truck to a halt in the parking lot and climbed out.

"Ready to do a canine lineup, Miss Holland?" Glade asked.

"I sure am."

They walked to the back of the truck. Rick said, "Officer, the Far North Veterinary Hospital is prepared to take some of these dogs in for medical care if you need a place."

"I'm sure we will," Glade replied.

Rick nodded. "We can take fifteen. But there are more than that out back, and another batch inside the building."

"Can you give me a list of other places that might take some?" Glade asked.

"Sure. I can recommend other veterinary practices and one or two *good* kennels."

Trooper Straski opened the back gate of the truck and called to Glade, "Want to help me lift these cages down?"

Rick hurried to help them, and soon the first cage sat on the pavement.

Robyn knelt beside it and peered in at the dog. "Oh, he's scared."

"Do you recognize him?" Rick asked.

She couldn't tell for sure through the small openings in the plastic cage. "Can we open the door?"

"We'd better get a leash first," he said. "If these people do train them to fight, the dogs might be aggressive when they come out of the cages."

"I think I saw a leash in the truck cab." Straski went to get it and returned with a red nylon leash in his hand.

"Okay," Rick said, taking the line. "Robyn, open the door slowly, and if he lets me, I'll clip the line to his collar. If he has one."

"What if he tries to attack you?" Glade asked.

Rick looked up into Robyn's eyes. "If I say, 'Shut it,' do it fast."

"Got it." Slowly she opened the cage door a couple of inches. The dog inside cowered at the back of the cage.

Rick bent cautiously to peer inside. "It's a white dog, smaller than Astro. Siberian husky, I think."

The dog let out a low whine. Robyn knelt, and he moved aside so she could look in. "Wocket!" A laugh bubbled up her throat. "That's Pat's other dog. He's small, but he's got heart and stamina."

"All right!" Rick grinned at her. "You can at least give your client good news today."

"Shall we leave him in the cage for now and look at the others?" Glade asked.

"Good idea." Robyn stood. "Rick, we may need to have you bring them home in your truck. We brought Mom's car into town today."

"Piece of cake," Rick said.

Glade had his notebook out but looked up from his writing. "I don't have a problem with you taking them in the cages if you want, Dr. Baker. You can return the cages to us when it's convenient—within the next few days."

"Thanks," Rick said. He and Straski hefted the next cage out of the truck. "This guy's heavier."

The dog in the cage shifted its weight and barked.

Hope clutched Robyn's throat. It sounded like the deep, insistent bark she'd heard every morning for the last two years when she went out to feed the male dogs at home.

"I think it's Hero."

"Okay. Let's play it safe and slow." Rick bent down, ready to grab the dog when the door opened.

Robyn couldn't help bouncing on her toes and smiling. "Ready?"

"Ready."

She cracked the door open, and the dog barked again. As soon as she saw his muzzle and ears push through the crack, she knew. "It's him! Take it easy, boy. It's me, so calm down."

Rick clipped the leash to Hero's collar.

She swung the door wide, edged around the cage, and dropped to her knees on the pavement. Hero catapulted into her arms and put his forepaws on her shoulders, the better to lick her face.

Robyn laughed and hugged him. "Okay, okay." She rubbed her face in his ruff of fur and stood. Hero jumped up on his hind feet and again rested his front paws on her shoulders.

"Oh, yeah," Rick said. "Somebody's glad to see Mom."

"He won't want to go back in the cage now," Robyn said.

Rick looked toward his truck. "I could put him in the cab of my pickup until we're ready to leave."

She nodded. "We can't let him loose, but I don't want to stuff him back in that cage until we have to. Come on, fella."

Rick unlocked his truck, and she led Hero to it. He hopped into the cab readily, and she stroked his thick fur.

"We're only going to leave you in here for a little while. I'll be back. And you can see us the whole time." Reluctantly, she shut him in.

Rick's smile was a bit lopsided. "He'll be okay."

"I know. I just hate to confine him again."

They went back to the confiscated truck. The two troopers had another cage ready to open. Inside was another of Robyn's dogs, Rounder. She let him prance around her on the leash for a few minutes and then put him back in the cage.

Only one more cage remained in the truck. Robyn gulped and eyed Rick. His troubled eyes mirrored her own dismay. They still lacked two stolen dogs, Tumble and Clipper.

When the troopers lifted the cage out of the truck, a low, guttural snarl issued from within. Robyn caught her breath. She couldn't imagine that noise coming from either of the two unaccounted for Holland dogs.

"Let's think about this," she said.

Rick leaned over the cage and peered into one of the slots. Snapping and growling caused him to jerk backward. "I think it's a bulldog."

eleven

"Oh, great," said Glade.

"An English bulldog?" Robyn asked.

"That or a pit bull, but he looks heavy."

"A couple of years ago we raided a dog fight," Glade said. "They were using bulldogs. Had a Rottweiler, too."

"Let's not open the cage." Robyn stood back, eyeing it warily.

Rick exhaled heavily. "Well, counting Astro, we've found four of your six."

"Here comes the warrant," said Straski. "Maybe your other two are inside."

"Let's hope so." Rick stepped closer to Robyn. "How are you doing? Are you cold?"

"A little." She flipped the hood of her parka up and stuck her hands in her pockets. The temperature had fallen several degrees since noon, and the sun was already falling toward the horizon.

"You and your mom will have to drive home in the dark."

Robyn shrugged. "We expect that this time of year."

As Straski took a radio call, two officers got out of the newly arrived cruiser and handed Glade a folded paper.

"Here's your warrant. You want us to stay?"

"Yes. We may need you to help us line up emergency care for several dozen mistreated dogs." Glade opened the paper and scanned it. He nodded, refolded it, and tucked it inside his notebook. "All right, I've got the suspect's keys here. Let's see how many mutts are in the building."

Straski walked over to Glade. "That call was from Joel Dawes. He said to tell you that they've been questioning Keeler. He claims someone brought the dogs to him yesterday, and he didn't know they were stolen. Supposedly the man said he wanted to board them for a few days until a sled race."

"Oh, right," Glade said. "Then where was Keeler taking them today?"

"No clue." Straski grimaced. "Dawes says to check his files and see if there's paperwork on the dogs in question. If there's any truth to Keeler's story, we should find the name of the person who brought them, which he's conveniently forgotten. But if Keeler went out to Wasilla and nabbed them himself, or if he's in it with whoever did the actual theft, we won't find it."

"Right. Or else we'll find falsified records." Glade unlocked the front door and opened it.

Rick and Robyn followed him and the other officers inside. Immediately a cacophony of barking erupted from the back room.

The tall trooper walked to the doorway and the noise level increased. "There's got to be two dozen dogs in there." Glade had to yell to be heard over the din.

"And that's not counting the ones out back," Rick said.

Glade squared his shoulders and took a deep breath. "Suppose you start writing that list of kennels and vets for me, Dr. Baker. Straski, you make a quick survey of the records out here. The rest of us will help Miss Holland see if her other dogs are in those cages."

They found several leashes hanging on nails inside the room. One by one, Robyn glanced into the cages and eliminated the dogs. At last she came to one that held an Alaskan husky, and her heart soared. "This is Clipper. He's mine."

"Is it safe to let him out?" Glade asked.

"Yes, he'll be fine."

The dog emerged from his confinement yipping and wagging his tail.

"Hush, now," Robyn said, but her smile almost split her

face. Only one more. *Thank You, Lord,* she prayed as she stroked Clipper's fur. *Please let us find Tumble, too.*

Fifteen minutes later they opened the last cage to reveal an Irish setter. Robyn's stomach twisted.

By this time, Rick had completed his calls and stood beside her. "I'm sorry," he said softly.

Glade frowned. "The one that's still unaccounted for— he's your top dog, right?"

Robyn nodded, unable to speak past the painful lump in her throat.

Glade riffled back through his notes. "And your most valuable. I don't know what to tell you, Miss Holland. We'll go through the pens out back to make sure, but I'm starting to think they got him out of here quickly."

One of the other officers said, "Could be they had a private buyer for him. Or maybe he was so tough looking, they took him straight to a fighting ring."

Robyn shuddered, and Rick slipped his arm around her. While she usually thought of herself as a self-sufficient woman, she welcomed his strength and warmth today. Knowing he truly cared about her and the dogs shored up her spirits.

"Let's look out back," she said to Glade.

Half an hour later—at almost four thirty—Robyn and Rick left with a sheaf of paperwork and five dogs. Astro, Rounder, Hero, Wocket, and Clipper rested in cages in the back of Rick's pickup.

As he drove directly to the restaurant where Robyn had left her car after lunch, she took out her phone and called Patrick Isherwood. "This is Robyn. I have some good news."

"You found the dogs. Tell me you found them."

She smiled. "Yes, we did. Pat, I'm so sorry this happened. But Astro and Wocket are fine. Astro has a small laceration on his front left leg, but it's superficial. We're in Anchorage, and a vet is going to thoroughly examine them. Then we'll take them home. They'll be back at Holland Kennel tonight."

"Bless you! I don't know what you did to find them, but I sure do appreciate it."

"Thanks." Her voice cracked a little. "The state police have arrested one man, and more may be charged. I'll call you again tomorrow and give you all the details."

While Rick pulled into the restaurant's parking lot, Robyn inquired about Patrick's health and signed off. She blew out a long breath, thankful he hadn't pressed her too closely about her own dogs. She didn't want to have to say it aloud yet, or to think the unthinkable—that Tumble might be lost forever.

"I'm so thankful we found most of them," she said to Rick. "I know you were praying the whole time."

"I was. I still am." He got out and opened her door. Slowly they walked toward her car. It had been a long day, and she felt like a wrung-out dishrag. Even so, she hated to end her time with him. "Thanks so much for being there. For everything."

"I'll have them home in a couple of hours." She noticed fine lines at the corners of his eyes and realized he was tired, too.

"Take your time." She gazed toward his truck. The dogs stayed quiet in their cages. She wanted to go take one last look at each of them, but that wasn't necessary. Rick would take the best possible care of them until they returned to their own spots at Holland Kennel.

"I don't want to keep them caged any longer than I have to," he said. "And it's cold. Even though we put blankets over the cages, I don't want to leave them in the truck long. I'll take them out at Far North and feed them and give them some water. And I'll look them all over in good light for wounds or any other problems."

"Astro's the only one we know of with an injury," she noted, "but if you see any serious problems and feel any of them need overnight care, call me."

Rick nodded. "I think Astro did that on the chain. Scraped his leg. Poor guy was pretty wound up, and very excited to see you. I don't think they hurt him intentionally."

"Ha. But they would have put them in a situation where they had to fight for their lives." Robyn scowled and shook her head.

"The police have no proof of that yet," Rick said.

"Well, the troopers did find a list of phone numbers for people who are known to be involved in dog fighting. Trooper Glade said so."

"Yes. And it's likely Keeler was delivering the dogs in his truck to someone connected with that. But they'll need more evidence before they can press charges. Meanwhile, they can charge Keeler with accepting stolen merchandise—"

"Merchandise!" Robyn snorted. "These dogs aren't merchandise. And I still don't understand why they don't charge him with theft."

"Patience," Rick said. "They're searching his house tonight. If they find a snow machine and trailer there. . .well, who knows what will come of this. But it may have been someone else who stole the dogs and took them to Keeler. He might be just a middle man."

"He's not as ignorant as he claims."

"Agreed." Rick smiled down at her. "Hey, you're shivering. Get that car warmed up and go pick up your mom. I'll bring the dogs to your house later."

"Thanks, Rick. I don't know how I would have made it through today without you." She stood on tiptoe and kissed him on the cheek, feeling very bold. The look in his soft brown eyes melted her heart.

"I'm glad I could help." He waved and headed for the pickup.

❧

Robyn paid special attention to the recovered dogs the next

day. All of them seemed healthy, and already Astro's wound looked better. Rick had treated it with an antibiotic salve that tasted bad enough to keep the dog from worrying at it.

Her mother didn't have to work, and they'd both stayed up late, settling the dogs into their kennels after Rick brought them home.

Robyn went into the barn after feeding them all breakfast and opened her training notebook. As she looked over her notations on which dogs had been exercised that week, she realized she was woefully behind on her training program, both for Patrick's dogs and her own team. The stolen dogs should have a light workout, she decided, except for Astro. After that, she'd take out a bigger team for a serious training run.

She took down the harnesses, checking her notes to be sure she got the correct size for each dog. Instead of having a set for each animal, she used color-coded harnesses in four sizes and kept a list in her notebook of which size fit each dog. Along with the four harnesses, she set out a short towline, four tuglines that clipped to a ring at the back of each harness, and four short necklines that connected each dog's collar to the towline.

As she gathered the pile of lines and set them on her plastic toboggan, her mother opened the barn door. "Trooper Glade called, and he's on his way here. He says he has some new information on that man Keeler."

"Okay. I was going to go mushing, but I'll wait."

Her mother nodded. "I figure it must be important or he'd have told me over the phone instead of coming out here."

Robyn tidied up her work area in the little barn and went into the house. Mom was puttering about the kitchen. Robyn sat down at her computer and checked her email. Several people had written to her with questions about the Fire & Ice 100 and the shorter races that would be held the same day while they waited for the long-distance mushers to complete the course.

"Mom, Dennis Cooper wants to know if we can board his team the night before the race. He's staying at the Grandview, but he needs a place for eighteen dogs, just for one night."

Her mom shook her head, her eyes widened. "Two weeks from today. Wow. I can't believe how fast it's crept up on us. I guess we have room. You'd know better than I would."

Robyn frowned and opened a spreadsheet on the screen. "We're taking Becky Simon's team. We'll be really crowded, but I don't blame them for wanting their dogs in a locked enclosure. We can shorten the tethers and squeeze in a few more for one night."

"Some people will sleep in their trucks and stay near their dogs," Mom said.

"Yes, but it's been brutally cold. Today's the first day we've had above freezing in weeks. If it's cold that night, people and dogs could get pretty uncomfortable."

Mom walked over to the desk and set a cup of hot tea down beside Robyn. "We could bring the puppies in for the night and put Dennis's team in the puppy yard."

"Hey, that's a thought. I'll tell Dennis we can take his bunch, but that's it, okay? If anyone else calls or emails, tell them we're overflowing. And thanks for the tea."

Glade arrived a short time later, and Robyn welcomed him into the living room.

"We've done some more checking on Philip Sterns," he announced.

"Could you connect him to the theft of the dogs?" Robyn asked.

"No, nothing solid. If he's behind it, he hired someone else to do it. He alibied himself in Anchorage that morning and has credit card slips from buying gas and lunch on his way here."

Robyn sank back in her chair and let the air *whoosh* out of her lungs. "When we heard he had a criminal record, I was sure he was up to no good."

Glade took out his notebook and flipped a few pages. "It looks as though he plans to make a fresh start here in Alaska, where few people know about his criminal past. We'll watch him, but for now we've got to give him the benefit of the doubt."

"I understand," Robyn said.

"What about Keeler?" her mother asked. "Did you get any more information out of him yet?"

"Some." Glade leaned forward and tapped the notebook with his pen. "The files at the kennel gave us some names, and some of the names are familiar to us."

"Did they tell you who took our dogs to him?" Mom asked.

He shook his head. "I strongly suspect Keeler was in on the theft. He'd entered the dogs in his ledger as new arrivals, but with a dummy client name and address."

"You searched his house, didn't you?" Robyn asked.

"Yes, and we found some circumstantial evidence." Glade turned to her mother. "Mrs. Holland, we found two snow machines and a trailer at Keeler's house, as well as several dog cages. That's not unusual in itself, and he does run a kennel. But I'd like to show you some pictures of the equipment and see if you recognize it. I knew you had Internet service, so I wonder if we can take a look at some photos I posted on the police page this morning."

Robyn took him to the computer, and Glade quickly brought up the Web site and keyed in the necessary coding to access the photos.

Mom studied the pictures pensively and shook her head. "I can't be sure. And I didn't get the license plate number. The color seems right, but I was looking more at the people on the snow machine."

"I've asked you this before, but was there one person or two?"

"I think there were two. I'm not a hundred percent sure. I saw them from behind as they drove away. I had the impression of a large person partially blocking my view of a smaller person sitting in front of him. I think it was the colors of their clothing that made me think it, because I couldn't distinctly see a second person." She shook her head. "I'm sorry."

"Based on the footprints we found near the snowmobile tracks, I think there were two people here that day, too." Glade looked at Robyn. "And you haven't found anything else since I was here Wednesday?"

"Nothing. I bought some extra locks in Anchorage yesterday though. We'll be extra vigilant between now and the Fire & Ice."

"That's the race your business sponsors?"

"Yes. It's two weeks from tomorrow."

"Well, I hope everything goes well for you." Glade stood and zipped his jacket. "I'll call you if we get any solid information in this case."

"The cages we used to bring the dogs home are out back," Robyn said.

"I can take them now, if you'd like."

Mom grabbed a jacket and followed them out the back door.

Robyn led them to the five stacked cages.

"Some of those were on the trailer the day the dogs were stolen."

Robyn looked at her mom. "Exactly like this?"

Her mother frowned. "I think so. Gray with red trim. Yes, I think they were just like these."

Glade ran a hand over the top of one cage. "These are probably sold in a lot of places."

"Yeah, it's a common brand," Robyn said. "Probably a lot of kennels use them."

"Well, it's a little something to add to the file we're building."

When he had left, Robyn returned to the dog lot and stood outside the fence, looking in at the male dogs. Wocket,

Max, and the rest whined and wriggled, eager to join her for a run in the snow. She prayed in silence, thanking God for returning the lost dogs to her. Their financial situation hadn't changed in the long run, though the cash from the dogs Sterns had bought would help some. In two weeks they'd know how much profit they realized from the race. But she felt at peace. God would take care of her and Mom, and Grandpa, too. In her mind, having the five powerful dogs back in her care was proof of God's love. Even though she feared she would never see Tumble again, God knew where he was. If it was part of God's plan for her and the business, Tumble, too, would come home.

She hurried to the shed and got the toboggan with the harnesses. In just a few minutes, her team of four was hitched to the new sled. She unclipped the snub line, grasped the handlebar, and called, "Hike!"

ॐ

Late that afternoon, when the sun dipped low toward the mountains, Rick drove from his humble office in downtown Wasilla to the Hollands' house. Cheryl directed him around to the back. He stopped at the edge of the dog lot and smiled.

Robyn and Darby were playing with several yearlings in the puppy enclosure.

"Hello, ladies."

"Hi, Dr. Baker," Darby said. "Look at what Bobble can do." She touched the puppy's head to focus his attention then moved her hand in a circular motion. The puppy flopped on his side and rolled over.

Rick laughed. "That's terrific. How long did it take you to teach him that?"

"This is only my third session working on it with him." Darby took a treat from her pocket and tossed it to Bobble, who caught it neatly in his mouth.

Behind him, the back door to the house opened. "Darby,

your mom just drove in," Cheryl called.

"Thanks, Mrs. H." Darby made a face at Robyn. "Gotta go. I'll see you at the meeting tomorrow."

"Okay. Thanks for helping." Robyn opened the gate just wide enough for her and Darby to squeeze through without taking any pups with them.

"Thanks for my mushing lesson," Darby called over her shoulder as she ran around the corner of the house.

"She's a good helper." Robyn bent over the gate and put two padlocks in place. Her loose dark hair spilled out of her hood and hid her features from him until she straightened. "She's going to be a great musher, too. I expect her to win the Iditarod or the Yukon Quest someday."

"I hope I'm there to see it. Are you busy?" Rick asked. "Is it time to feed this motley crew?"

She smiled. "Not yet. In about an hour."

"Take a ride with me?"

"A sled ride?"

Rick chuckled and reached to brush back a strand of her hair. "No, I meant in my truck. If we hurry, we can get up on the ridge behind my house and see the sunset."

"Sure. Just let me tell Mom." Her flicker of a smile left him with an impression of shyness as she jogged to the back door.

She was back a moment later, and he reached for her hand. They walked together in silence to the pickup in the driveway. His own property was only a quarter mile down the road, and he turned in at the gravel drive to his log home. The house was silent as they drove past it, but smoke oozed from the chimney.

Rick shifted into four-wheel drive, and they bounced up the hill behind the house on the track he'd packed with his snow machine. The shallow snow had compressed enough for him to drive to the top of the ridge without danger of getting stuck.

When he stopped the truck, he put it in park and left

the engine running. The view of the town and the highway couldn't be beat, and he traced the part of the trail he could see, where the racing teams would compete for the trophy in two weeks. But the distant mountains and snow-covered plains glistening in the late rays of sunlight drew his gaze and dazzled him. As he and Robyn watched without speaking, dusk shrouded the mountainsides in deep purple and gray. Pink, gold, and red reflected off the peaks.

Robyn sighed. "I could never leave Alaska." She cast a quick glance his way, and her forehead crinkled, as though she feared she'd said the wrong thing.

"I love it here, too," he said. "Especially out in the wild. I was smothering in Anchorage. That's why I moved out here last year—to be closer to the land but still near enough to civilization that I could earn a living."

Her expression cleared and they sat in silence, watching the colors spread and change. As the shadows of night overtook them and the mountain peaks dulled to shades of gray, she stirred. "When the race is over, I hope I'll be able to get out on the trail more myself."

"Maybe we can take another run together soon." Rick smiled at the memory of their sledding adventure earlier in the week. It had started as a perfect day. Cheryl's news of the theft had derailed it fast though. He hoped they would be able to spend more days together—carefree days. And soon.

Robyn smiled up at him. "I'd like that a lot. You're pretty good at mushing."

He pulled in a deep breath and decided now was the time to express the burden on his heart. "Robyn, I've been praying for you and your family. I want you to know that I'm confident God has some solutions for you. To your financial situation and your grandpa's health problems. God knows all about it. He already knows how He's going to resolve those things."

She put her fingertips gently to his cheek. "Thank you."

Her gaze flickered away but came back to him. "Do you think I did the wrong thing yesterday? To chase around hunting for the dogs, I mean."

"I hadn't even considered it. That's not at all what I meant."

She nodded, her eyes wide and attentive. "I was afraid afterward that I'd overstepped some boundary."

"I don't think so. We'd all been praying about it. God used your persistence to bring the dogs home. If you hadn't gone looking for them, perhaps He'd have used another means. Or maybe He'd have let them all slip away and never be found. We don't know, do we?"

"No, we don't. You're right—the Lord knew all along He would take us to them and let us bring them home. I've tried to rest in Him about Tumble and the other unresolved issues. I'm so thankful we got five of them back. And I'm glad you were there, too. When I told Mom about it, she was horrified at what I'd done. She kept saying, 'If you'd gone there alone, that man might have killed you.'"

"I doubt that," Rick said, but the thought sobered him. "Robyn, I love the way you are."

Her eyelids flew up, and he chuckled.

"I love your passion for the dogs, and your confidence in your skill. But I also love the fact that you can be impulsive now and then."

She laughed. "Are you sure?"

"Okay, not *too* impulsive. But, yeah. Yesterday I was a little frustrated when you wouldn't give up the search. But I admired you for that, too. You're really something, and. . .and I like that something."

Her cheeks took on a becoming flush.

He held her gaze for a long moment. "There's something I want to tell you."

Her eager gaze encouraged him to go on.

"I'm tired of running back and forth to Anchorage."

She frowned and her lips parted. "You. . .just said you love it out here. You're not going to move back there, are you?"

"No. I need to stop working at Far North. It's not fair to the folks in Wasilla. I want to have a full-service hospital for the animals here and be open every day, with the assurance that pets can stay there if they need recovery time and monitoring."

"What are you going to do about it?"

"I've told the partners at Far North that it's too hard for me to keep coming into town. I'm going to stop seeing patients at the clinic altogether at the end of the month."

"What did they say?"

Rick toyed with his key ring. "Hap and Bob aren't thrilled with that, and I admit I've enjoyed working with them. I learned a lot during the five years I was in practice with them. But it's time."

"Will they bring in a new doctor to take your place?"

"They'll have to," Rick said. "Bob plans to retire next year. But I'm not going back."

Her smile reached deep inside him, and he blurted the rest of his plan. "I'm thinking of advertising for a partner, too."

"Really?"

He nodded. "There's enough business, and if we have two doctors, one of us could always cover emergency calls. I'd need a bigger building. I've looked around some, but I haven't found anything suitable that I could rent, and my current landlord doesn't want to add on to the building I'm renting." He hesitated then shrugged. "I'm thinking of building an animal hospital beside my house."

"Wow. Are you sure you'd want to be that close to it?" Robyn sat up straighter and gazed down the hill toward his log home.

"I don't know. It would be convenient, but I can picture it becoming burdensome, too. I'm praying about it. I'd like to have a place big enough for some kennels and an area where I could treat large animals."

Her face took on a glow of excitement in the twilight. "That would be terrific. But expensive."

"I know. I think I can swing it within a couple of years. And I know exactly what I want for the building." He pointed down the hill to a flat area across the driveway from his house. "Right down there. That's where I want it. The bank is looking at my loan application. This is my home now, and I want to build my business here, too."

"I think that's wonderful." Her dark eyes caught the gleam of the last rays of sun off the snow.

Rick reached for her without another twinge of hesitation. As the long darkness settled about them, he kissed her, delighting in her response. He no longer wondered if she might be the right woman for him. Rick had found his home and the one he hoped would share it with him.

twelve

The *Anchorage Daily News* ran its article about the Fire &
Ice race on the following Wednesday. Robyn had granted
permission for them to lift photos from the Holland Kennel's
Web site.

"Hey, this looks great," her mother said as Robyn came in
from giving the dogs their breakfast.

Robyn poured herself a cup of coffee and joined her at the
kitchen table. "Let me see."

Together they perused the article.

"That's one of their pictures from last year's race." Robyn
pointed to a photo of Pat Isherwood crossing the finish line
with his arms raised over his head in victory.

"They took the one of you from our site," Mom said. "I've
always liked that one."

Robyn grimaced. "I should put some new ones up, I guess.
That picture's about three years old. Oh, look here. They
pulled the one off the 'puppy page.'" The photo near the
bottom of the story showed Grandpa Steve in the dog lot,
his arms brimming with husky puppies.

"This is a fantastic article," her mom said. "They never
gave us this much publicity before."

"Maybe the news about the dog theft last week helped."
Robyn shuddered. "Makes me feel kind of weird."

Robyn's phone rang, and she answered it.

"Hey, Robyn," Darby squealed in her ear. "Did you see the
paper?"

"We're looking at it now."

"Isn't that Bobble on the right in the picture with your
grandfather?"

Robyn laughed. "It sure is. Coming over after school?"

"I'll be there."

Darby clicked off and Robyn closed her phone, but her mother's phone rang almost immediately.

"Hello? Who?" She made a face at Robyn. "I think you want to speak to my daughter." She held her phone out and hissed, "It's someone from the *Seattle Times*."

"The Seattle. . . ?" Robyn gulped. She'd half expected to hear from the weekly papers or the *Mat-Su Valley Frontiersman*, but not the huge daily paper in Seattle. "May I help you?"

A woman's voice said, "I saw the story in the *Anchorage Daily*, and I'd like to interview you."

Robyn stared at her mother and said into the phone, "You want to know about next week's race?"

"Well, sure, you can tell me about that, but I mostly want to know about you. The woman who runs Holland Kennel and chased down the thugs who stole her sled dogs."

"Uh. . ." She held the phone away from her face. "Mom, they want to interview me."

Her mother pushed her chair back. "Go for it, honey. People outside Alaska will hear about the race."

Any publicity would be good for the business, Robyn told herself, though she disliked having the spotlight shine on her. She gulped and smiled. "I guess that's all right," she told the reporter. Of course, it was silly to wear this plastic smile when the woman was fifteen hundred miles away. She felt like an idiot. She lost the smile in a hurry, before Mom turned around and saw it.

❦

Rick closed the door of his small veterinary office at five o'clock on Saturday. He checked his hair in the rearview mirror before heading for the Hollands' house. Maybe he should stop at home first and clean up a little. But Robyn had said to come as early as he could. Her brother, Aven, and his wife had arrived, and Rick was invited to share supper with the family.

Robyn met him at the door and drew him into the house. A tall, dark-haired man in uniform rose and waited for her to introduce them.

"Rick, this is my brother, Aven," Robyn said with a smile and a fond glance toward the young man.

Rick extended his hand and shook Aven's, feeling as he did so that Robyn's brother was assessing him.

"Glad to meet you," Aven said. "Mom and Robyn have told us a lot about you."

"Nothing bad," Robyn said quickly.

Rick smiled. "I've heard a few tales myself. I think the family's glad to have you home."

"They're staying all week, until after the race." Robyn couldn't seem to stop grinning. Rick loved seeing her so happy. She looked toward the hallway as a pretty young blond woman wearing black pants and a red sweater entered the room. "Oh, and this is Caddie, my sister-in-law. Caddie, this is Rick Baker."

"Pleased to meet you, Dr. Baker." Caddie took his hand.

"Oh please, let's not go all formal or I'll have to learn your ranks," Rick said.

Aven and Caddie laughed.

"Agreed," said Caddie. "Let's not go there. I just changed out of my uniform, and I'm ready to relax for a few days and be just plain Caddie."

Rick doubted she had ever been considered plain, and the pride in her husband's eyes confirmed that.

"What are your jobs for the race?" Rick asked as they settled down to talk.

"I'm the jack-of-all-trades," Aven said. "I've worked on every one of these races since Dad and Grandpa started it twelve years ago—except for last year and the year before. Couldn't get leave. But I've missed it, and I worked it out months in advance so that Caddie and I could be here for this one."

"I agree with Aven," Caddie said. "I'll do whatever is needed. Someone may have to explain things to me, since I've never gotten involved in dog sled racing, but I'll take lots of pictures, and I'll help wherever I can."

"Don't worry," Robyn said. "We'll put you to work."

❧

On race day Robyn could hardly contain her joy. The start area near Iditarod Headquarters came to life at five a.m., when volunteers opened the check-in and service booths and the contestants began readying their teams. As race director, Robyn dashed from one task to another. The six o'clock starting time approached at lightning speed. All the checkpoints were manned by several volunteers, and all the drop bags of extra supplies, equipment, and food for the dogs and mushers had been delivered to the stops along the route.

As usual, the Fire & Ice trail would begin and end in an open area near the Iditarod Headquarters building. Trucks, booths, contestants, volunteers, and spectators turned the grounds into a temporary, dog-centered city, not unlike some of the tent cities that had sprung up during Gold Rush days.

"Slow down, girl," Grandpa called as Robyn passed where he sat in a wheelchair, near the starting line.

She laughed and paused to kiss his forehead. "I'm so glad you're here, Grandpa."

"I wouldn't miss this for anything." He pulled her closer and added, "And I'm not going back to that place."

"I hope you never need to." She tugged his hood up over his knit hat. "I'll help you with your therapy every day."

"Robyn, a photographer's here from the *Frontiersman*," Aven called. "Do you have time to speak to him?"

"Uh, not really." Robyn lifted her hands helplessly. "Point him toward Billy Olan. He's one of the favorites today, since Pat Isherwood isn't well enough to race yet. Oh, and

Rachel Fisher's team looks good. She and her dogs are very photogenic."

Aven led the photographer away, and Robyn blew out an exaggerated breath.

"Aw, you're photogenic, too, Robbie." Grandpa grinned up at her.

"Thanks. I love getting publicity for the race, but I hate having the attention focused on me."

"Hey, you're still going to let me hand the trophy to the winner, right?" he asked.

"Yes, of course." She squeezed his thin shoulders. "Are you cold, Grandpa? I can help you go inside for a while if you need to warm up."

"Not yet. I'm warm as toast." He held up one hand, clad in a hand-knit woolen mitten. "Your mother made sure of that this morning."

Robyn laughed and hurried to the registration area.

The volunteers greeted her.

"All of the mushers have checked in," Anna said, handing her a clipboard.

"Great." Robyn scanned the list. The forty-eight dog teams comprised a record number of contestants. Rick and his old partner, Dr. Hap Shelley, had examined all the entered dogs the day before. Now the mushers harnessed their teams and gathered near the starting line.

"We've got three entries who've previously run the Iditarod," Anna said with a dreamy smile, "and so far I've seen two Iditarod winners in the crowd."

"I hope there'll be more before the race starts," Robyn said. "I'm counting on at least four." More good publicity when the big-name mushers turned out to support the race.

Aven dashed to the booth. "Robyn, Mom wants to know if we have any extra booties handy."

"Booties?"

"For Erica Willis. She had a slight mishap on the way here

and some of her equipment got wet. Her dogs need eight dry booties."

"Sure." Robyn told him where to find the needed accessories for the dogs. "Oh, and did all the drop bags get delivered to the halfway point? I never got confirmation on that."

"We're all set," Aven said over his shoulder as he hurried away.

"How you doing?"

She whirled and found Rick standing behind her. "Terrific. How about you?"

"Ditto. This is great fun."

"It's a madhouse," Robyn conceded, "but I love it."

He handed her a loose-leaf binder. "All pre-race vet checks are complete. Hey, isn't that—"

Robyn turned to look at the man who'd snagged his attention. She caught her breath. "Philip Sterns."

"Thought so."

She and Rick waited as Sterns wove through the crowd toward the booth. It took him only a couple of minutes to locate them. "Miss Holland. Good to see you again."

"I'm surprised to see you here, Mr. Sterns," she said.

He smiled and nodded at Rick. "I returned from California yesterday and thought I'd come up here to watch the race. Maybe get some inspiration for training my new team." His brow furrowed. "Say, have you heard anything about those dogs you lost?"

Robyn studied his face for a moment. "Yes. We got most of them back."

"Oh? That's good news." He looked around as though expecting to see the dogs popping up out of thin air. "Did you get that magnificent Tumble back?"

Robyn glanced at Rick. His sympathetic gaze told her the interview was painful for him, too. "No, actually we recovered all of them except Tumble. The police are still hoping to find him."

Sterns nodded, his eyes wide. "I wish you the best."

"Thank you. Now, if you'll excuse me, the race is about to start."

The teams entering the 100-mile race gathered near the start area. Ormand Lesley, the race marshal, called the time for the first racer, and the team took off to the sound of much cheering. At two-minute intervals, the other teams set out over the trail in the pre-dawn darkness.

Robyn wished she was driving a sled today, following the trail away from the crowd, out into the quiet tundra.

The spectators cheered each team on its way then settled down to watch the shorter races.

As soon as all of the teams in the 100-mile race had left, Rick approached Robyn again. "Guess I'd better jump in my truck and get to the halfway checkpoint."

"Have fun." She wished she could go with him and watch the teams come into the rest stop one by one, but she was needed here. "We'll see you later."

He smiled at her. "Save me some coffee."

She waved and grinned as he drove out. The sled teams would all take a two-hour rest at the fifty-mile point, and during that time, Rick and another vet would examine each dog. If all were in good condition, after their mandatory halt they could head on back to Wasilla and the finish line.

By ten o'clock, the sun had risen and the temperature climbed to a comfortable twenty-five degrees. People took their folding chairs and waterproof cushions to the edge of the trail where the other races would be run during the time that the long-distance teams were gone.

Robyn didn't expect the winning team to cross the line before mid-afternoon. The record time for the Fire & Ice, not including the required two-hour stop, was seven hours and twenty minutes. But that was not a terribly fast time, and it was always possible someone would knock the record to smithereens. They probably wouldn't see any sleds come in until well after three, but everyone would start to get keyed up and watch the trail eagerly from two o'clock on.

During the morning, short runs for teams of four, six, and up to ten dogs were held on shorter trails nearby. Each team completed two heats, and their times were added together. In each class, the dogs' route was as many miles long as the number of dogs allowed per team. A two-dog class for children ages twelve and younger was a favorite feature of the day's program. That class ran only a mile for each of its two heats.

People ate lunches they'd brought or bought snacks from the vendors. One of the past Iditarod winners gave a talk about the historic race inside the headquarters building, and spectators viewed the exhibits there and visited the gift shop.

All too soon the sun began to lower in the west. Robyn hoped the first teams of the 100-mile race would come in before it set. Pictures of the finish would be better, and the spectators would get a bigger thrill from the event if they could see well.

At two forty five, Ormand Lesley called her via radio. Cell phones just didn't make the grade where the race went.

"The leaders just passed the last checkpoint," Ormand said. "It's Olan and Fisher in a tight race."

Robyn's pulse quickened. If Rachel Fisher won, it would be a coup for Holland Kennel. She wouldn't be the first woman to capture the trophy, but half her team was sired by Holland dogs, with four of Tumble's offspring among them.

"They're ten miles out," she announced to those nearest her. "Olan and Fisher leading."

Darby jumped up and down and clapped her gloved hands. "Oh, I hope Rachel wins it. We haven't had a member of the local sled club win for three years."

Robyn smiled. "Yeah. It sounds like she has a good chance."

The buzz mounted as word got around. Robyn went to the

speaker and made the official update. "Folks, we'll be seeing the first finishers in just a few minutes."

Spectators hurried to get refreshments before the real excitement began. The participants in the shorter races tended their dogs and put away their equipment.

Aven and Caddie found Robyn. "Hey," her brother shouted. "Want to come in the truck to where we can see the lake?"

"I sure do." They would be able to see the teams coming across the frozen lake from a hill a short distance away. Robyn looked around. "Where's Grandpa?"

Caddie said, "Your mom took him inside to warm up and have something to eat, but they'll be out here when the leaders come in. Aven promised to radio in when we see them."

"Oh, let me come, too." Darby seized Robyn's arm and bounced on her toes.

Robyn laughed. "All right, but you'll have to sit on my lap."

The four of them piled into Aven's pickup. In just a couple of minutes they gained the vantage point and looked down on the windswept lake.

Caddie shivered. "It's getting cold, now that the sun is going down."

"I see them!" Darby pointed, and they all followed her gesture, squinting against the glare of sun on snow.

At the far side of the lake, a team of sixteen dogs ran down the bank and onto the glare ice. The sled's runners had barely hit the surface when a second team appeared and plunged down the bank after them.

Robyn held her breath.

"Who's leading?" Aven asked.

"I can't tell. Should have brought binoculars." Robyn frowned in concentration.

"I've got a zoom lens." Caddie held up her camera and peered through the viewfinder. "Can't read the bib number."

"That's Rachel!" Darby grabbed Robyn's hand and laughed.

"See her red hood? It's Rachel for sure. Billy Olan's wearing dark green."

They watched in silence as the two teams skimmed over the lake. Billy's fourteen dogs gained slowly on Rachel. As his leaders came up to her sled and veered out around her team, Rachel bent low. The watchers faintly heard her call to her dogs. They put on a new burst of speed and maintained their lead all the way across the ice, though not increasing it.

When they reached the near side of the lake, Rachel's team bounded up the bank and out of sight into a stand of trees on the shore. Billy's team ran after her.

"Let's go back," Aven said. "We don't want to miss it when they cross the finish line."

They squeezed into the truck. Robyn took the radio and called her mother as they barreled down the hill to the paved road and back to the race's finish area.

Mom and Grandpa were just coming from the head-quarters building, and Robyn ran over to update them. "Mom, I think Rachel might win it. She was barely ahead of Billy when they crossed the lake. I'm so excited for her!"

"I'll be disappointed if she loses now," Darby said.

Grandpa looked eagerly toward the finish line. "No matter where she places, she's run a good race."

"Yes. I'm thinking she and Billy might both break the race record." Robyn chuckled in delight. "I hope that guy from the *Frontiersman* is still here."

"He's inside eating doughnuts," Mom said.

"Yes, I let him interview me about the history of the race." Grandpa nodded and leaned on his daughter-in-law's shoulder. "Come on, Cheryl, I need to get back to my chair and sit down."

The crowd stood three-deep along the lane roped off to form the finish. Grandpa sat to one side just over the line, with the rest of the Holland family close by. The throng roared and cheered as the teams came in, but the dogs trotted on until they crossed the line and the mushers called, "Whoa." Caddie and the news photographer snapped away with their cameras.

Rachel Fisher brought her team in just seconds before Billy Olan's. Rachel set her snow hook and fell into her excited husband's arms.

Aven used the portable speaker to draw the people's attention and handed the microphone to Robyn.

She waited for the crowd to quiet. "The winner of this year's Fire & Ice 100 is Rachel Fisher of Wasilla."

Cheers erupted once more.

"Her leaders are Canby and Soot. Her trophy will be awarded tonight at the banquet. And in second place, we have Billy Olan of Talkeetna. His lead dogs are Buster and. . ." Robyn checked her clipboard. "And Sitka."

Out of the corner of her eye, she saw a police car enter the parking area.

thirteen

Robyn couldn't help feeling a tiny bit annoyed as her anxiety level climbed. They didn't need police officers making the people nervous. Probably they were just checking to make sure everything stayed orderly with a crowd this size.

The trooper got out of his vehicle and sauntered toward them.

Robyn thrust the microphone into her brother's hands. "Take over. That's Trooper Glade, the officer who investigated the dog theft."

She walked quickly toward Glade, thankful to hear Aven launch into an update on the other contestants: "We've just received word by radio that a third team is within a mile of the finish."

The crowd's attention was diverted in the opposite direction from Robyn and the trooper as they strained to spot the next team.

"Hello." She held out her hand and Glade shook it. "Is there any news for us?"

Her mother joined them and greeted Glade.

"I do have a bit of information that should interest you. I'm sure you remember the man who bought some dogs from you the day of the theft."

"Philip Sterns," Robyn said, nodding.

"Yes," the trooper said.

"He's here."

Glade's eyes widened. "Here, as in right here this minute?"

Her mother turned and scanned the spectators. "He's been here all day, hobnobbing with the racing folk. I last saw him over on the right side of the finish line."

"Do you know what his vehicle looks like?" Glade asked.

Mom shook her head.

"Probably a rental again," Robyn said. "I didn't notice it when he arrived."

"Are you sure he's still here?"

"Ninety-nine percent. I saw him about three minutes ago."

"All right," Glade said. "Hold on a sec. I'm going to call this in. If you see him moving toward the parking area, please alert me immediately."

He walked toward his car, and Mom said, "What do you suppose this is about?"

"No clue." Robyn chewed her lower lip.

Behind them, the crowd began to clap and shout as another dog team sped toward the finish.

A few minutes later, the people hushed again and Aven announced the third-place finisher.

Glade again got out of his car and came toward them. "Sorry to leave you ladies in the dark, but I wanted to be sure my backup is nearly here. I expect another officer in about ten minutes." He looked at Robyn. "You met my backup at the kennel the day we recovered the other dogs—Trooper Straski."

Robyn pounced on the one word that gave her hope. "*Other* dogs?"

Glade grinned. "We found the last one."

"You—" Robyn seized her mother's wrist and looked over her shoulder. "This has something to do with Sterns?"

"It has a lot to do with Sterns. We figured your lead dog had been passed to a fighting promoter or sold out of state already, but we decided to check a few more kennels, just in case. But nothing turned up. Until today, that is."

"What happened?" Robyn asked.

"Remember the kennel where Sterns parked the other dogs he'd bought from you?"

"Yes. Rick and I talked to the owner the day after the theft."

"She called our switchboard yesterday and asked for an officer to come around."

"Tumble was there?" Robyn stared open-mouthed at her mother and shook her head. "He certainly wasn't there the day we went in."

"That's right. I believe the kennel owner was totally innocent. She said Sterns came back for his three dogs a few days ago and asked if she could take them again this weekend while he drove up here for the race. And he said he'd added a fourth dog and would leave all of them, if she had room."

"I left her my card and asked her to call me if she heard anything about Tumble or stolen sled dogs," Robyn said.

Glade smiled in sympathy. "We'd also told her to call us if anything suspicious happened. Maybe she knew you'd be busy with the race today."

"You mean she just accepted his word and let him leave the dog without any questions?" Robyn asked.

"She said she recognized Tumble immediately because she'd looked at his pictures so many times over the past two weeks. Sterns showed her a veterinarian's certificate, saying the dog was up-to-date on his shots, but it had a different dog's name and registration number, though the general description was close enough to get by. She didn't let him know she suspected it was Tumble."

"Good for her," Mom said.

Glade nodded. "After he left, she got on your Web site and compared the pictures of Tumble to the new dog he'd brought her. The resemblance was enough to make her call us."

"You're certain it's Tumble?" Robyn asked.

"Absolutely. When Straski compared the pictures of your missing lead dog with the real thing, he could see it was either Tumble or a ringer. Since you'd told us the day he was stolen that your dogs all had microchip implants for identification, our next step was to get someone to read the microchip. The Humane Society was able to help us, and we verified that it really is your dog." Glade stiffened, focusing on something behind them. "Heads up. I think I see Sterns moving this way."

Mom's eyes widened. "What do we do?"

"Nothing. Just stay calm, and don't turn around unless he comes over here and speaks to one of us." Glade glanced over their heads. "He sees me."

"Well, those hats aren't exactly camouflage," Robyn muttered.

Glade cracked a smile. "Oops. He's changed course and is heading for the parking lot. Excuse me, ladies." He jogged away from them, and Robyn turned to watch. Sure enough, Philip Sterns was walking swiftly past a row of parked vehicles.

"Go get Aven," she said to her mother. She followed Glade slowly, watching as the trooper angled to intercept Sterns.

A familiar pickup entered the parking lot just then, and Robyn caught her breath. Rick was returning from the halfway checkpoint, which meant all the mushers had left there. He pulled in slowly and scanned the rows of cars.

Sterns reached a dark green SUV and opened the driver's door. Glade hurried across the lot, but Sterns already had the vehicle in motion and backed out of his parking space.

Robyn watched helplessly from her vantage point forty yards away. If only Rick knew what Glade had just told her.

Glade's shout reached her ears, but Sterns paid no attention to him. He quickly shifted the transmission and plowed forward with his SUV, forcing Glade to leap aside to avoid being struck down.

Rick's pickup went into a quick reverse and turn. Robyn's heart leaped. He must have seen what was happening. As he positioned his truck sideways across the lane between parked vehicles, she sent up a frantic prayer.

Sterns barreled toward him but hit the brakes at the last possible moment. Instead of slamming into Rick's pickup, the SUV slowed, skidded on the snowy surface, and gently smacked the pickup's rear passenger-side fender. Rick's truck spun a quarter turn in the lane, and both vehicles came to rest.

Before either man could get out of his truck, Glade reached Sterns's door. "Get out of the vehicle! Keep your hands high."

Another police vehicle came into the lot and stopped just beyond Rick's truck. Trooper Straski got out and hurried to help Glade.

Robyn walked over to where Rick was climbing out of his pickup. "What's going on?" he asked. "I saw that guy almost run Glade down and figured I could block the exit, but I didn't realize it was Sterns until just now."

"They've found Tumble. And they've got proof that Sterns was involved."

Rick's jaw dropped and he opened his arms.

She launched herself into his embrace.

"Thank You, Lord." Rick hugged her, then stood back and looked toward the side of his truck. "Looks like I'll need to call my insurance company."

"I'm just glad you showed up when you did," Robyn said, "and that you reacted quickly enough to stop him. If he'd gotten out onto the road, it could have meant a high-speed chase."

Rick exhaled heavily. "Yeah. That wouldn't have been so good."

Aven came running from the area near the finish line with Caddie and his mother close behind. "What's up?" Aven called. "Did the police get him?"

Robyn looked over to where Glade was putting Sterns in the back of his cruiser. "They sure did."

"One of us had better get back to the booth," Caddie said regretfully. "We left Darby to announce the teams as they come in, and things are happening fast over there."

"I'll go back with you," Aven said, smiling down at his wife, "but we want all the details later, you hear me?" He fixed Robyn with a phony glare, and she was able to raise a smile.

"Don't worry about that. We'll tell you every little thing tonight."

"Grandpa's probably going nuts," Mom said, looking anxiously toward where they'd left him.

"We'll probably have to tell this story several times." Robyn grimaced. "You can tell him they've found Tumble and caught Sterns and that I'll give him the blow-by-blow as soon as I can."

Aven and Caddie hurried back toward the race area.

Straski approached Robyn, her mother, and Rick. "Well, folks, this could have ended worse."

"Yes," Mom said. "Thank you so much."

Straski spread his hands. "I'm the latecomer." He nodded at Rick. "I understand you did some fast thinking and driving, Doc. Good job. If you'll step over here, I'll take your statement. We've called for a tow truck from town to come take Sterns's vehicle away." He eyed Rick's truck. "Yours looks drivable."

"Yes, I intend to drive it to a garage for an estimate," Rick said.

Robyn and her mother added what little they could to the officers' reports with their accounts of Sterns's appearance at the race.

"Why on earth did he come here today?" Robyn asked.

Glade shook his head. "You got me. Maybe he wanted to establish himself as a friend of yours—a satisfied customer—so you wouldn't suspect him anymore."

Rick said, "Or maybe he was establishing an alibi for another crime."

The officers were silent for a moment then Glade said, "Interesting theory. Maybe we'd better check around and see if any major thefts happened today—especially where sled dogs are concerned."

"When will you question him?" Robyn asked.

"He's already talking." Glade looked at his notes. "I told him I'd picked Tumble up at the kennel this morning and that we've arrested three people connected to the Barkland place. We've got strong evidence they've been supplying dogs for fighting. When I told him all that and named the men who actually stole your dogs, he admitted he got Tumble from them."

"He hired them to steal the Hollands' dogs?" Rick asked.

"He hasn't confessed to that. . .yet," Glade said. "He'd like me to believe they contacted him and he saw himself as Tumble's rescuer."

"Oh, right. That's why he told us he'd found him." Robyn shook her head in disgust.

"He will confess," Straski put in. "I talked to headquarters about fifteen minutes ago. Keeler named him as his client. Seems Sterns hired Keeler and his friends to steal Tumble. He told them they could have any other dogs they nabbed—he only wanted the one breeding male."

"Where's Tumble now?" Rick asked.

Robyn's pulse surged. "Yes, is he still in Anchorage?"

Straski grinned. "Step this way, madam. I have a passenger who's eager to see you."

Robyn grabbed Rick's arm to compensate for her wobbly knees. "You. . .have him here? Now?"

Straski laughed and turned toward his state police truck. He opened the back and rummaged for a moment. He took out a leash, rummaging a bit more as Rick and Robyn approached. When they were only a couple of yards away, he said, "Come on, fella. It's okay."

A whine emerged from the back of the truck.

"Tumble?" Robyn almost couldn't believe it was true, but when his furry black-and-white face poked out of the cage and he yipped with joy, she laughed. "Yes! Come on, Tumble."

The dog jumped down from the back of the truck and into her arms. She scooched down and hugged him, fluffing his fur. Tears filled her eyes.

A moment later she felt Rick's hand on her back. "What do you say I go tell you brother and ask him to make an announcement?" Rick asked.

"I'd like that." Robyn stood and held the leash firmly with both hands as Tumble pranced around her. "Ask him to tell everyone that Tumble has come home."

ॐ

After the awards banquet, the school cafeteria where the event was held emptied quickly. Soon the parking lot emptied.

Rick dived into the cleanup with the other volunteers. He managed to catch Cheryl alone for a moment when she went to fetch her father-in-law's coat and hat. "I don't know if Robyn told you, but I'm planning to expand my practice here in Wasilla," he said.

"She mentioned it. I think it's wonderful." Cheryl smiled. "Everyone here will be glad to know you're in town anytime they need you."

"Eventually I want to build a bigger facility and maybe even bring in a partner to work with me, but for now I think full-time hours and possibly adding a receptionist will move me forward."

He could tell the exact moment she latched onto his idea. Her eyes lit and she stared at him for a moment before speaking. "A receptionist?"

"Yes. I wondered if. . .well, I know you have a job, but I think you'd be an asset to my practice, Cheryl. I need someone to answer the phone, schedule appointments, keep records, and occasionally help me with the animals. Starting the beginning of February."

She was still staring at him. "Do you mean it?"

"Of course."

She laughed and hugged him. "Did you know how much I hate my job at the store? Standing up for hours on end?"

"Well, you could sit at least half the time, I'm sure. And when I build the new animal hospital, you'd be a lot closer to home. I plan to put it next to my house."

"Oh, Rick. I think. . .no, I *know* I adore you. Thank you so much."

Contentment worked its way through him. "I don't know what they pay you, but I'd try to at least match the hourly rate—"

"You had me with 'an asset to my practice.'"

He laughed. "Great. We'll talk over the details soon."

"I'll look forward to it."

"Mom?" Robyn made her way toward them. "Grandpa wants to know what's keeping you."

Cheryl threw a knowing glance at Rick. "I'm going to let this handsome veterinarian tell you." She hurried away.

Robyn watched her. "What's up? She looks radiant."

He chuckled. "Hope you don't mind. I just offered your mother a job."

"A job?"

"As my receptionist."

Robyn stood still for five long seconds. Rick was afraid she was upset, but slowly her lips curved upward. She leaned toward him. "Thank you. That's the most wonderful thing you could have told me, now that Tumble is found."

Rick reached for her hand. He hoped he'd have the courage to tell her a few more things soon. "Come on. Let's get this job done," he said.

The volunteers stripped the tables and tidied the serving area.

Aven and Caddie stayed until after nine o'clock, but finally Robyn pulled her brother aside. "Take your wife home. She looks exhausted."

Aven looked over at Caddie, a deep furrow creasing his

brow. "She does look beat. But we're almost finished here."

"I'll help Robyn lock up," Rick said. "We'll probably be only twenty minutes behind you."

"Okay." Aven looked at the pair uncertainly.

Rick winked at him. "We'll be fine. We just need to box up a few things and load them in my truck."

"All right. Want us to take Tumble?"

Rick looked over to where the dog was snoozing on the floor under one of the tables. He'd had his time in the spotlight earlier, and the race-goers had lavished attention on him. Rick fully expected to see Tumble's photo on the front page of tomorrow's newspaper.

"Sure," Robyn said. "Hitch him up in his kennel, would you?" Rick had taken her home earlier to feed all the Hollands' dogs, but she hadn't wanted to leave Tumble there so they'd brought him back. He'd behaved himself and sat quietly during the dinner.

Robyn called to him. He jumped up and trotted eagerly to her. "Go with Aven." She patted his head and smiled into his trusting eyes. "You big lug." She stooped and kissed the dog's forehead.

When Aven and Caddie had left with Tumble, Rick began packing up the last few things. "All of this goes to your house, right?" He gestured to the dishes and leftover paper plates and cups remaining on the nearest table.

"Yes, and those extra napkins. Oh, and Anna left her purse. I called her as soon as I found it, and she said she'll come pick it up tomorrow."

"And Patrick's taking his dogs home at last?"

"All eight of them go in the morning. I'll miss them."

Rick closed up the carton he had filled. "You'll lose a couple more soon, too, won't you?"

"Yes. I had two people come to me today and ask if I had team dogs they could buy." She smiled, but her eyes drooped.

"Sounds like business is doing almost too well."

"Yeah. It won't hurt us to thin out the ranks a little though. We'll have more puppies in spring, and I'll have a lot of youngsters to train. And Clay Brighton wants me to do some initial training with a litter of yearlings he has."

Rick nodded. "I'm proud of you."

"Thanks. I hope Grandpa feels well enough soon to start helping me again. I guess you heard Trooper Glade say we might be able to get back the three dogs Sterns bought. They're putting them in official custody at the kennel in Anchorage until after Sterns's arraignment. Aven thinks we should pursue it, and he's offered to help out if we suffer financially because of it."

"He's a good guy, your brother."

"The best."

A few minutes later, Rick began carrying cartons to the truck while Robyn held the door for him. At last the hall was cleared.

Robyn walked to the light switches. "Well, that's over for another year."

Rick put his arm around her and walked her to the door. A beam of light came in through the glass from a security light outside. "Tired?"

"Yeah. But not as tired as Grandpa."

"I hope he didn't overdo it today," Rick said.

"Me, too." Robyn fumbled with the key ring in her hand. "I'm a little concerned about Caddie, too."

"Oh? Something I don't know?"

"Maybe. She's expecting in August."

"Wow. I didn't know that." Rick couldn't help grinning. "That's terrific. Aven seemed awfully happy, but I just figured that was his normal, sunny personality."

She laughed. "I've never seen him this happy. Caddie's the best thing that ever happened to him."

Rick touched her cheek and looked into her eyes in the dimness. "I love it when you laugh. You're so beautiful then." He gulped. Would she think that meant he didn't find her beautiful at other times? Because he did, always. "Robyn. . ."

She didn't speak but arched her eyebrows and waited.

He hesitated only a heartbeat. "I love you."

She caught her breath and he pulled her into his arms. He kissed her as he'd wanted to for weeks, holding her close and running his hand through her thick, glossy hair.

"I love you, too," she whispered when he released her.

"There's so much we need to talk about."

"Whenever you're ready."

He pulled her close and held her for another minute, then took the keys from her. They stepped outside and he locked the door.

❧

In mid-April Rick arrived in the Holland Kennel dog yard as Darby finished her mushing lesson. He helped Robyn and Darby unhook the three dogs from the sled and put them away. As he pushed the sled, laden with harnesses, toward the shed, a snowball hit him in the back and he jumped about a foot off the ground.

"Gotcha!" Darby laughed.

He whirled in time to see her bend for another handful of snow. "Oh no, ya don't!" Rick scooped up enough to pack a quick snowball and lobbed it at her.

Robyn joined in and caught Darby on the arm. For a couple of minutes they exchanged shots, with Robyn alternating her aim between him and Darby.

At last, Rick held up both hands, laughing. "I surrender."

"Okay, Dr. Baker, I'll let you go this time, but only because I need to get home. Don't forget who's the champ though."

"Right. I'll get you next time. If there's enough snow left."

Darby headed for the driveway. "Thanks, Robyn. I'll see you tomorrow at church."

Rick helped Robyn put the equipment away in the shed. "The snow's going fast. Pretty soon you'll be training with the ATV again."

"I know." She smiled ruefully. "Grandpa wanted to drive again today. His last sled ride for the season. I let him take one ten-year-old dog inside the fenced yard. I feel so bad that we can't turn him loose with a team anymore."

"Maybe he'll get distracted this summer, helping you and working with all those new puppies."

"I hope so." She smiled up at him. "Where are we going tonight?"

"That new restaurant on the Goose Bay Road."

"Great. Anna says it's really good. Give me fifteen minutes to change?"

"Sure." They walked to the back door, and Rick held it open for her.

"Hi, Rick," Cheryl said as they entered the kitchen. She and Grandpa Steve sat at the kitchen table together.

"I'm going to change, Mom, and then we're going out to eat."

"Join us for a cup of tea while you wait, Rick?" Grandpa asked.

"Thanks, I'd like that." He removed his gloves and unzipped his jacket. Robyn headed off to her room, and Rick sat down beside her grandfather.

"Twelve of Tumble's new pups are reserved. Can you believe that?" Steve's eyes glittered. "We've only got four more babies, and Robby wants to keep two of them."

"I guess you'll stay busy this summer."

"You bet I will, Doc. Robyn plans to run the Iditarod next year, and I've been going over her plans with her. Gotta make sure all her equipment is just right, you know."

Rick nodded. "I'll be there to help."

Cheryl placed a mug of tea before him. "It's a big venture."

Grandpa nudged the sugar bowl Rick's way. "It is, but she can do it. She's a spunky girl. If she's not in the top ten, I'll eat my mukluks."

Rick laughed.

They were still discussing the big race when Robyn swept into the room wearing a calf-length skirt, an aqua sweater, and tall boots. "What are you yakking about now, Grandpa?"

"Our plans for the Iditarod, that's what."

She patted his shoulder. "That's right. We've got lots to do, haven't we?"

Rick stood. "Ready to go?"

"Yes." Robyn stooped to kiss Grandpa and blew her mom a kiss. "We won't be late."

"Well, we might be," Rick said.

"Oh?" She eyed him suspiciously.

"I'm not worried," Cheryl said. When Robyn turned to get her coat, she winked at Rick. "Have a good time, kids."

An hour and a half later, when they left the restaurant, the sun was just going down.

Robyn sat beside him in the truck, relaxed and dreamy. "What a beautiful night." She gazed out toward the mountains. The clouds glowed pink and lavender.

Rick drove to the lakeside park and stopped the truck where they could look out over the still-frozen expanse. "Hope you don't mind. I wanted to talk about something in the restaurant, but it seemed a little too popular."

"Yeah, it was crowded. The food was good though." She looked up at him with serious, dark eyes. "What did you want to tell me?"

"Not tell you. Ask you." He reached in his pocket and took out a small, square box. "I. . .I got you something when I was in Anchorage Monday. That is. . ." He hauled in a deep breath. Time to start over. "Robyn, I. . ."

She was staring at the little box. Slowly, her eyelashes lifted and she met his gaze but said nothing.

"I love you," he whispered.

Her lips quirked into the gentle smile he adored. "I love you, too."

He nodded, wondering if his no-frills plan was the best

after all. Robyn wasn't a lace-and-roses girl, but it wouldn't have hurt to buy some flowers.

She sat quietly beside him. Most women would have pounced on the box by now, squealing and crying. Not that she didn't care deeply, but she waited for him to do this his own way. So, what was his way?

The simple approach. He reached for her hand. "Will you marry me?"

Her sharp intake of breath left him in suspense for several seconds. Finally she exhaled.

Had he asked her too soon? She'd known for months how he felt. Was she wondering about all the things he'd pondered the last few weeks—what their home and businesses would look like, for instance, where all her dogs would reside, and how they'd make sure Grandpa Steve could live at home as long as possible?

"Yes."

"You will?"

"Nothing would make me happier than to be your wife."

He kissed her tenderly, nearly exploding with thankfulness and anticipation. The questions faded into the fast-falling dusk.

He drew back and placed the box in her palm, closing his hand around hers. "I made some guesses—educated ones. I hope you like it. But if you don't—"

She sprang the catch and held the box up close to her face. "Oh, Rick, how could I not like it?"

He helped her remove the ring and slid it onto her finger. "It's Alaskan gold and amethyst."

"It's perfect." She curved her arms around his neck. "Thank you for picking it."

He kissed her again.

"Mom and Grandpa will be so happy," she whispered in his ear.

"Yeah, they are."

She leaned back. "They are?"

"Uh. . .yeah. Your mom saw the box on my desk, and. . .I hope you don't mind. They're waiting for the official word."

She smiled and stroked his cheek. "Let's go."

epilogue

On a bright July day, Rick and Robyn stood together before their pastor at the little church in Wasilla. In the front row sat Cheryl, Steve, Aven, and Caddie. On the other side were Rick's parents and sisters, who had flown in for the wedding.

Anna and Darby stood beside Robyn at the front of the church. Because of her impending due date, Caddie had gently refused to be a bridesmaid. Rick had called on his brother and Bob Major for the occasion.

Friends, neighbors, owners of Rick's patients, and people in the sled dog business filled the church. Several renowned mushers slipped in anonymously before the ceremony, though the reporter from the *Frontiersman* spotted a couple of Iditarod winners and snapped photos of them entering the church.

Robyn held a lacy handkerchief to her eyes for a moment. Why should she cry? She was barely leaving home. She'd be living a quarter mile down the road from Mom and Grandpa, in Rick's snug log home. The dogs would stay at the Holland Kennel, and she could walk over every day to work with them.

Her mother had blossomed in her new position as receptionist at the Baker Veterinary Practice. She'd surprised and delighted Rick by organizing his records and transforming the atmosphere of his little office from chaotic to peaceful. When the new animal hospital was built, Rick and Robyn fully expected her to reign as office manager.

"What token do you give this woman?"

Robyn realized her thoughts had wandered.

Rick spoke up firmly. "A ring."

They both turned to gaze down the aisle. Darby's little sister, Katy, came proudly down the aisle with her eyes glittering. Wearing a snow-white harness and leash, Tumble walked beside her, lifting each foot daintily and gazing at the people in the pews.

When they reached the front of the church, Rick's brother knelt and detached a small box from Tumble's harness and handed it to Rick. He winked at Robyn and handed the box to the minister.

The pastor opened the box and revealed their wedding rings. Katy led Tumble to the side. She stood beside Darby and Anna and signaled to Tumble. He sat down and panted quietly, looking over the crowd.

A few minutes later, the vows were complete. Robyn gazed up into Rick's tender eyes as the pastor said, "You may kiss your bride."

As her husband bent and kissed her, Tumble let out a low bark. Darby and Katy both reached to pat him.

"Hush," Darby whispered. "You'll see her every day."

A Letter To Our Readers

Dear Reader:

In order that we might better contribute to your reading enjoyment, we would appreciate your taking a few minutes to respond to the following questions. We welcome your comments and read each form and letter we receive. When completed, please return to the following:

Fiction Editor
Heartsong Presents
PO Box 719
Uhrichsville, Ohio 44683

1. Did you enjoy reading *Fire and Ice* by Susan Page Davis?
   ❏ Very much! I would like to see more books by this author!
   ❏ Moderately. I would have enjoyed it more if

   _____

   _____

   _____

2. Are you a member of **Heartsong Presents**? ❏ Yes ❏ No
   If no, where did you purchase this book? _____

   _____

3. How would you rate, on a scale from 1 (poor) to 5 (superior), the cover design? _____

4. On a scale from 1 (poor) to 10 (superior), please rate the following elements.

   ____ Heroine   ____ Plot
   ____ Hero   ____ Inspirational theme
   ____ Setting   ____ Secondary characters

5. These characters were special because? _____

_____

_____

6. How has this book inspired your life? _____

_____

_____

7. What settings would you like to see covered in future

   Heartsong Presents books? _____

_____

_____

8. What are some inspirational themes you would like to see

   treated in future books? _____

_____

_____

9. Would you be interested in reading other **Heartsong Presents** titles? ❏ Yes ❏ No

10. Please check your age range:

   ❏ Under 18   ❏ 18-24
   ❏ 25-34   ❏ 35-45
   ❏ 46-55   ❏ Over 55

Name _____

Occupation _____

Address _____

City, State, Zip_____

E-mail _____

WHITE MOUNTAIN BRIDES

Journey home to New
Hampshire along
with three women
who survived years of
captivity among the
Native Americans and
now seek family, faith,
and love.

Fiction/Christian/Romance paperback, 352 pages, 5¾6" x 8"

Please send me ____ copies of *White Mountain Brides*. I am enclosing $7.97 for each.
(Please add $4.00 to cover postage and handling per order. OH add 7% tax.
If outside the U.S. please call 740-922-7280 for shipping charges.)

Name _____

Address _____

City, State, Zip _____

Presents

___HP773 *A Matter of Trust*, L. Harris
___HP774 *The Groom Wore Spurs*, J. Livingston
___HP777 *Seasons of Love*, E. Goddard
___HP778 *The Love Song*, J. Thompson
___HP781 *Always Yesterday*, J. Odell
___HP782 *Trespassed Hearts*, L. A. Coleman
___HP785 *If the Dress Fits*, D. Mayne
___HP786 *White as Snow*, J. Thompson
___HP789 *The Bride Wore Coveralls*, D. Ullrick
___HP790 *Garlic and Roses*, G. Martin
___HP793 *Coming Home*, T. Fowler
___HP794 *John's Quest*, C. Dowdy
___HP797 *Building Dreams*, K. Y'Barbo
___HP798 *Courting Disaster*, A. Boeshaar
___HP801 *Picture This*, N. Farrier
___HP802 *In Pursuit of Peace*, J. Johnson
___HP805 *Only Today*, J. Odell
___HP806 *Out of the Blue*, J. Thompson
___HP809 *Suited for Love*, L.A. Coleman
___HP810 *Butterfly Trees*, G. Martin
___HP813 *Castles in the Air*, A. Higman and J. A. Thompson
___HP814 *The Preacher Wore a Gun*, J. Livingston
___HP817 *By the Beckoning Sea*, C. G. Page
___HP818 *Buffalo Gal*, M. Connealy
___HP821 *Clueless Cowboy*, M. Connealy
___HP822 *Walk with Me*, B. Melby and C. Wienke
___HP825 *Until Tomorrow*, J. Odell

___HP826 *Milk Money*, C. Dowdy
___HP829 *Leap of Faith*, K. O'Brien
___HP830 *The Bossy Bridegroom*, M. Connealy
___HP833 *To Love a Gentle Stranger*, C. G. Page
___HP834 *Salt Water Taffie*, J. Hanna
___HP837 *Dream Chasers*, B. Melby and C. Wienke
___HP838 *For the Love of Books*, D. R. Robinson
___HP841 *Val's Prayer*, T. Fowler
___HP842 *The Superheroes Next Door*, A Boeshaar
___HP845 *Cotton Candy Clouds*, J. Hanna
___HP846 *Bittersweet Memories*, C. Dowdy
___HP849 *Sweet Joy of My Life*, C. G. Page
___HP850 *Trail to Justice*, S. P. Davis
___HP853 *A Whole New Light*, K. O'Brien
___HP854 *Hearts on the Road*, D. Brandmeyer
___HP857 *Stillwater Promise*, B. Melby and C. Wienke
___HP858 *A Wagonload of Trouble*, V. McDonough
___HP861 *Sweet Harmony*, J. Hanna
___HP862 *Heath's Choice*, T. Fowler
___HP865 *Always Ready*, S. P. Davis
___HP866 *Finding Home*, J. Johnson
___HP869 *Noah's Ark*, D. Mayne
___HP870 *God Gave the Song*, K.E. Kovach
___HP873 *Autumn Rains*, M. Johnson
___HP874 *Pleasant Surprises*, B. Melby & C. Wienke
___HP877 *A Still, Small Voice*, K. Obrein
___HP878 *Opie's Challenge*, T. Fowler

Great Inspirational Romance at a Great Price!

Heartsong Presents books are inspirational romances in contemporary and historical settings, designed to give you an enjoyable, spirit-lifting reading experience. You can choose wonderfully written titles from some of today's best authors like Wanda E. Brunstetter, Mary Connealy, Susan Page Davis, Cathy Marie Hake, Joyce Livingston, and many others.

When ordering quantities less than twelve, above titles are $2.97 each.
Not all titles may be available at time of order.

SEND TO: **Heartsong Presents** Readers' Service
P.O. Box 721, Uhrichsville, Ohio 44683

Please send me the items checked above. I am enclosing $ _____
(please add $4.00 to cover postage per order. OH add 7% tax. WA add 8.5%). Send check or money order, no cash or C.O.D.s, please.

To place a credit card order, call 1-740-922-7280.

NAME _____

ADDRESS _____

CITY/STATE _____ ZIP _____